P9-DDR-741

"Suspense and character move this psychic quest novel along smoothly for an excellent read."

—*Denver Post* on *Witchlight*

"The plot is appropriately shivery. . . . Bradley offers quite a few surprises in the writing."

—*The San Francisco Chronicle* on *Ghostlight*

"A master of science fiction and historical fantasy, Bradley proves herself equally adept at contemporary fantasy with a Gothic twist. Mixes parapsychology with the occult and strong characterizations."

—*Library Journal* on *Gravelight*

"This gifted writer once again introduces the extraordinary into daily life. This novel is Bradley at her best. *Witchlight* is a well-told tale full of mystery and wonder, centered around characters whose realism makes it easier to believe in the fantastic."

—*Rapport*

"That mage of magic, Marion Zimmer Bradley, will take you truly elsewhere in *Ghostlight*. Fascinating . . . Bradley's tales may not begin 'Once upon a time . . .' but they have that ambiance, the suspension of disbelief, the immersion in story which is the hallmark of all good [fairy tales]. This is no exception."

— *Rockland Courier-Gazette*

"Bradley's large fandom will be pleased."

—*Booklist* on *Heartlight*

Witch Hill

MARION ZIMMER BRADLEY

A TOM DOHERTY ASSOCIATES BOOK

NEW YORK

WITCH HILL

Copyright © 1990 by Marion Zimmer Bradley

A Tor Book
Published by Tom Doherty Associates, LLC
175 Fifth Avenue
New York, NY 10010

www.tor.com

Tor® is a registered trademark of Tom Doherty Associates, LLC.

Library of Congress Cataloging-in-Publication Data

Bradley, Marion Zimmer.
    Witch Hill / Marion Zimmer Bradley—1st Tor trade paperback ed.
      p. cm.
    "A Tom Doherty Associates book."
    ISBN 0-312-87283-6 (acid-free paper)
    1 . Inheritance and succession—Fiction.   2. Massachusetts—Fiction.
3. Young women—Fiction.   4. Witchcraft—Fiction.   5. Witches—
Fiction.   6. Aunts—Fiction.   I. Title.

    PS3552.R228 W48 2000
    813'.54—dc21   00-028653

First Tor Mass Market Edition: November 1990
First Tor Trade Paperback Edition: September 2000

Printed in the United States of America

0 9 8 7 6 5 4 3 2 1

for Jonathan Frid
and
Barnabas

A NOTE FROM THE AUTHOR

The towns of Witch Hill and Madison Corners, with all their inhabitants, exist only in the imagination of the writer; the cities of Arkham and Innsmouth, and Miskatonic University, were created by H. P. Lovecraft. The characters in the book are all imaginary; if the name of a real person is used, a little thought will tell the reader that any name a novelist can invent must at some time have been given to somebody on this overpopulated planet. So if your name is used, it isn't intended to be you.

M. Z. Bradley

Witch Hill

ONE

A PLACE TO LAY MY HEAD

IT BEGAN TO RAIN JUST AS THE FUNERAL LIMOUSINE DROVE OUT OF the cemetery, and all the way back into the city, the hard beating of the rain and the steady swish-swish-swish of the wipers ran counterpoint to my own dismal thoughts. A week ago, there had been four of us. Four Latimers. Mother—Janet Latimer—fragile and often ill, which is why I had given up the exciting work I was doing at the Art School, and come home to look after her; but alive and very precious, well worth the coddling and care to save her failing heart any stress. Father—Paul Latimer—still vital, still very erect and slender, his hair greying but his eyes as bright as ever and his voice strong and definite. And Brad, the way he had looked in his uniform as he boarded the train to Parris Island for basic training; just nineteen, so full of fun and laughter.

A tight little circle; a loving family, but not a smothering or stifling one. I'd been on my own for three years, until Mother's heart attack, and I would be again when she was stronger. Brad had always wanted to go into the Marines; there'd been a Latimer in the armed forces ever since the Revolutionary War. Oh, we had lives of our own—but we had roots, too, and a strong, firm family. When Brad stepped on the train, the family wasn't breaking up; it was just loosening the apron strings; he'd go away from home as a gawky kid, as I'd gone away from home a shy teenage girl, and he'd come home a grown man, as I'd come home an adult, even a sophisticated woman, sure of the direction I wanted my life to take.

Only none of it had happened. Like a row of dominoes, as if we'd been set up for some idiot force to flick us with a finger, one after another, we'd gone down. It began with the yellow telegram from Brad's commander, and the words that had all run together in front of my eyes: *Regret-to-inform-you—your-son-Paul-Bradley-Latimer-IV—killed-in-crash-of-training-helicopter*—and the name I never could decipher or remember. My first thought, and Father's, had been: *Mother—she mustn't know yet. It will kill her.*

It did. She came in while the thought was still clear on our faces and before we could get the telegram out of sight. She said, in a whisper, "Is it Brad?" and even before we could answer or try to delay or deny it, dropped, like a stone. In the emergency room they said she must have been dead before she struck the floor, while Father and I were still racing to pick her up.

Riding in a funeral limousine just like this, four days ago, Father had spoken—almost for the first time—of his own roots. Among other things, he said we used to be related to half of Massachusetts. All I knew about his early life was that he'd been born in a little town in New England, near the coast; and that he'd left it at the age of sixteen, for reasons he never discussed. I didn't even know the name of the town; but that day he'd said, holding on to my hand, "Sara, when I die, I want to be buried here, beside your mother. Don't let anyone talk you into taking me back to Arkham, no matter what anyone in my family might say."

"Your family? I never knew—you never mentioned anyone, Father."

"No, I didn't," he said. "I suppose—well, I kept putting it off, year after year, telling you. I suppose, like most children, you just took it for granted that there were a few generations between you and Adam. I always thought there'd be plenty of time—that I'd go back some day. After Aunt Sara died—my father's sister, she died seven years ago—I always intended to go back some day and make my peace with all of them—or as many of them as were still alive; they're probably all dead now. But I thought I'd give everyone time to forget I'd ever existed. And then it turned out that there wasn't any time."

I picked up the name. "An Aunt Sara? Was I named for her, Father?"

He smiled bleakly. "No, Sara," he said, "but I was in the Marines—in Japan, as it happened—when you were born. So I left it to your poor mother to name you, and of all the infernal names in the calendar, she had to pick *Sara*—not that I'm blaming her, of course—Sara was her roommate's name at college. But *Sara* was—the one name I would never have given you!"

"Why not, Father?"

"Some other time," he said, and flinched. "No, not that. We've had a lesson in how little time any of us have—well, honey, let's put it this way. There has always been a Sara Latimer in our family, and none of them have been very happy, or very lucky. The first Sara Latimer was hanged for a witch, in Arkham, almost three hundred years ago. And ever since then—are you superstitious, Sara?"

"I don't think so. No more than anyone else." I said it quickly, not really thinking; I didn't worry about spilled salt, or walking under ladders, didn't cringe at the idea of black cats and didn't read my horoscope in the newspapers—or if I did, it was only to giggle. "No, not at all."

My father had smiled, sadly. His face was lined, and it seemed suddenly that he had aged twenty years in the last four days. With a small shudder of terror, it struck me; he was past sixty. *And now he was all I had. . . .*

"I never believed in superstitions, either; nor in bad luck, or family curses, or any of that sort of rot. Except—well, I was born in Arkham, and brought up to all kinds of stories about our family's history, talk about family curses, especially all the various Sara Latimers and the way they'd all met with violent deaths—oh, yes, that was part of it, too. I never mentioned any of it to your mother, and before you were born I gave her *carte blanche* to name you anything she liked. I sort of thought a little Janet would have been nice. But she picked Sara—just coincidence of course; but when I read her letter, there in HQ in Okinawa, I tell you, the cold chills ran up and down my spine."

"Strange," I said thoughtfully, "there are so *many* names in the world—"

"Well, Sara is a popular name," Father said slowly, "but when I heard she'd chosen to name you Sara, it seemed to me it was like the old saying about lightning. They used to say, when I was a boy in New England, that lightning never strikes twice in the same place. But it *does*. It's even *more* likely to strike where it's struck before. Our old house on Witch Hill Road was at the very top of a hill, and *every* summer, almost every thunderstorm, lightning would strike there, usually the northwest corner of the house. After we had electric lights put in, when I was ten years old or so, it seemed as if every storm struck the transformer outside, and my father finally had the lights disconnected; so we went back to using lamps and candles. Said it wasn't worth the danger of setting the house on fire, just to sit up and turn night into day. As I remember, Aunt Sara was pleased—she never did like the electric lights anyhow."

I, too, felt a small cold chill running up and down my spine. Lightning had struck twice in our family, indeed, already. And how could I count on it never striking again? "Is that why you never called me Sara when I was little? I was 'Sissy' until I went to school, and Sally after that, until I got into high school. Mother called me Sara, but you never did."

"That's so," he agreed, "the name stuck in my throat, so to speak. I'd gone so far to keep my daughter from being one of the Latimer— uh—from being a Sara Latimer," he amended. "And it seemed like Fate had just stepped in, no matter how I felt about it."

It was a gloomy enough conversation, it seemed; and yet, even to me, it was better than letting our minds turn back—back to the cemetery behind us, where Mother and Brad lay side by side. It would be bad enough to go back to the apartment alone. Maybe I could persuade Father to come away for a few days; perhaps to revisit the family of which he never spoke. I said, as lightly as I could manage, "Don't tell me that all the Sara Latimers went to the devil—and I don't believe in the devil. Not even in Arkham. After all, there aren't any witches, and haven't been for a couple of hundred years— even in Arkham!"

"I'm not so sure," he said somberly. "Anyway, they were all a pretty bad lot. There are a lot of Latimers up that way—Latimers and Marshes, my mother was a Marsh. You're related to half of Vermont and Rhode Island. Respectable folks, all of them, mostly farmers, blacksmiths, a few parsons, now and again some girl who'd get away to normal school—teachers college, you'd say nowadays—and come back to turn schoolmarm. Stubborn folks, too. Been me, *I'd* never have named another girl Sara after the first one was hanged out there on Witch Hill. But the old family Bible—I used to look in it, when I was a kid, went back to the seventeen-hundreds or something—had a Sara every couple of generations, and just as often as a Sara turned up in the family, she'd mean trouble." My father was not even talking to me now; his eyes were distant, and his voice had taken on the remote up-country twang which he had educated himself out of decades before. He was thinking out loud, not telling me family history. "One, two of the Saras died real young—babies in arms. But the rest, regular; Sara Jane Latimer; drowned, 1812. Sara Lou Latimer; died in childbirth, age sixteen, 1864. *She* ran off with a Confederate soldier. Sara Anne Latimer; killed by dogs, 1884. And one, Sara Beth,

I don't rightly know just what she did, but they erased her name from the family Bible, and you had to be pretty wicked for that to happen!"

"No wonder you believed in the family curse," I said. "It does sound fairly—ominous. What about my Aunt Sara, the one I *wasn't* named for?"

His face hardened again. "Your Aunt Sara," he said slowly, "was one of the worst. She made my father's life hell, and my mother's, and mine. When I told her I was leaving, and taking my mother with me, she told me I'd come to a bloody bad end, and I swore that I'd never set foot in the same state with her so long as I lived. And I never have. That's why—"

The limousine's brakes screeched; I jerked forward, clutching wildly at the armrest. Then there was a huge, crunching, shattering, smashing sound, a scream from somewhere, and a terrible cry, and the world went out. The last thing I saw was my father's face, with blood slowly flowing down over an unmoving eye; then it, too, vanished.

When I came to in the emergency room of the hospital, they didn't have to tell me that he was dead. All through the hours of unconsciousness, the words—almost his last words, after all—had seemed to echo in my mind.

She told me I'd come to a bloody bad end . . .

All the Sara Latimers met a violent death . . .

The color of blood, the smell of it, the confused images of violence and savage death and cursing, made slow whirling pictures in my mind.

It turned out that there was nothing wrong with me but a mild concussion, an inch of skin scraped off my right leg, and assorted cuts and bruises; but my father had been flung, as the car spun, into the center of the expressway; two or three cars had passed over his body before they could stop. They advised me not to see his body, and they kept the newspapers away from me, in the hospital; but I saw a headline on somebody else's paper, COLLEGE PROFESSOR KILLED EN ROUTE HOME FROM DOUBLE FAMILY FUNERAL. I didn't read it; I just turned my face to the wall, and I let them bury him in a sealed coffin. And now, for the second time in a week, I was riding home from the cemetery, and the rain was falling on the graves of Paul Bradley Latimer III, Paul Bradley Latimer IV, and Janet Soames Latimer, and I was almost hoping that this funeral limousine would do the same stunt as the last one I rode in. What the hell—! Lightning always strikes twice, three times, and all the Sara Latimers had met with a violent death and there was just room, out there, for one more damned grave.

The rain kept pouring down, and I stared gloomily out at the wet streets slipping by. The hard, burning pain in my head, half unhealed concussion and half unshed tears, throbbed on. The driver, in the front seat, drove with slow, meticulous care; I suppose he'd been especially cautioned not to let the lightning strike twice at his own place of employment. A macabre thought drifted into my mind—was he afraid they'd think he was drumming up more business?—and to my own horror I heard myself giggle; the driver twitched and half looked around.

"You all right, Miss?"

I mumbled something noncommittal and hoped he'd think it had been a sob or that I was hysterical. Damn it, why shouldn't I laugh? My mother and father had laughed more than anyone else I'd ever known, and if they were anywhere and could feel anything at all—not that I had any hope of that—they'd hate to see me sitting around crying. Could they know, or care, whether I laughed or cried on the way back from their funeral, or were the God-is-Dead crew right after all, and would they never know or care about anything for the rest of eternity?

Dismally, staring at the rain, I wished I had some kind of definite faith. I didn't even know what my father or mother had believed. Once

my father had said—not to me, but to a colleague at his university—
that he'd heard enough religion to make him sick, as a kid: that he'd
turned allergic to it. Although full of good will for his fellow man, I
never had heard him express an opinion, one way or the other, about
immortality or the afterlife. My mother had taken us to Sunday
school when Brad and I were little, but she almost never went to
church herself, and seemed to have no particular commitment to it.

Not that this was particularly strange, in the circles we moved
in; religion was the one thing nobody ever paid any attention to, and
nobody seemed to feel the lack. I'd discussed it, a little, during my
time at the Art School; most of my friends had been brought up
without it, as I was, and although we didn't know quite what we *did*
believe in, we knew what we *didn't.*

I could no more imagine either my father or mother, or Brad, sitting up on a cloud, with wings and playing a harp, than I could
imagine them tossing in an old-fashioned pit of brimstone. Conventional hells didn't seem to make much more sense, in this century,
than conventional heavens. I wished I could think of my family still
existing somewhere, even if not in any conventional heaven; but I
neither believed nor disbelieved. Quite frankly, I didn't know. And
now, when I needed and wanted to know, there was nothing but an
empty place inside.

The funeral parlor's limousine drew up in front of the shabby
red-brick building where we had had our five-room apartment since
Brad got too big to have his crib in my bedroom, fifteen years ago.
The driver shielded me tenderly from the rain with an umbrella until I was inside the vestibule, and when I took out my key, unlocked
the door for me.

"You'll be all right, now, Miss? You're not going to be alone? Listen, don't you have a friend you can call to come and stay with you?"

I reassured him, and watched him climb back in the limousine
and zoom away. Poor guy, he was in a gloomy business. I pushed the
elevator button and got out, used the inside key, and went inside,

steeling myself to get through the bad evening that lay ahead. No, there was no one I could call to come and be with me. My high school and junior college friends were all married or moved away. The friends of the last three years were three thousand miles away, in California, and none of them had been close enough to come that far—I hadn't written to any of them since I came back East. Not even to Roderick, because I knew I'd either have to marry him, or think up another good reason for *not* marrying him, this time.

The lights were still on where Father and I had left them on to go to Mother's funeral; he had said, "We wouldn't want to come back to a dark house." I swallowed hard again, and went out in the kitchen to make myself a cup of tea. It was bad, out there. Mother's blue-and-white smock—she hated aprons—was still hanging on the hook behind the refrigerator. I'd done most of the housework, these last few months, but the doctor had warned me that she hated feeling useless, so I'd let her do anything light enough to put no strain on her heart. Her hand-crocheted potholders were hanging on the stove by the little magnets she sewed inside them.

Four Latimers and I was the only one left. Sara Latimer. *None of them were very lucky.* Why had my father left his home? I'd never know, now. He hadn't even finished his story about his Aunt Sara.

I filled the copper teakettle and put tea leaves in the pot, but when the kettle whistled, I realized that tea wasn't what I wanted. Tea was too much of a family ritual—my parents had both been coffee-haters, so that the family's panacea, like the chicken soup which had become a joke about Jewish mothers, was a huge hot cup of tea, liberally sugared and, when Brad and I were little, diluted with milk.

Whenever, as a child, I'd failed in an exam, come in wet and cold from skating, or depressed from a tiresome day, whenever we gathered in the kitchen before bedtime, the big old stoneware pot had been brought out, and Mother had said soothingly, "There, there, I'll make you a nice hot cup of tea and you'll feel better." I found myself on the point of another fit of hysterical giggles; there *couldn't* be an afterlife, or wherever she was, Mother would hear me crying, and whisper a ghostly "There, there . . . it's all right, Sara, you'll feel better after you have a nice cup of tea . . ."

Resolutely I poured the boiling water down the drain, walked into the living room, opened the sideboard and brought out a bottle of Scotch. It had never been opened; Dad had kept it for rare guests and had really liked tea better, or orange juice. I tilted a generous dram into the teacup I found still in my hand, tipped it up and drank. It went down, burning, then strangely warm and soothing. I poured another.

The doorbell rang. I jumped—who on earth would be coming out now, in the rain? Carrying drink and bottle, I went to the door and opened it. Come on, lightning, strike three times, what the hell, maybe it's the Boston Strangler.

The mild, disapproving face of Mr. Patterson, who owned the building—all five floors and ten apartments of it—moved from the cup in my left hand to the bottle of Scotch in my right. "Er—Miss Latimer, if you have a minute—"

"You've know me fifteen years, you can still call me Sara," I said carelessly. "As you see, I'm having a drink. Will you join me?"

He stepped inside. He kept on casting sneaky little glances at the bottle of Scotch. Did he think I was an alcoholic drowning my sorrows? But when I repeated my offer he shook his head. "Oh, no. No, thank you. No, too early for me, really. Look, I'm sorry to intrude on you at such a time—"

"Is the rent due? I'd forgotten what day of the month it was. For that matter, I've forgotten what month it is."

"Oh, no. Not at all. I wouldn't—I mean—no, but I suppose— you do know that the lease on this apartment is up at the end of this month? I don't suppose you've had time to make plans yet, but—will you be wanting to renew? I mean, a young woman, all alone, I mean, that is, a single woman—"

I took pity on the tactless wretch. "It's all right," I said, as if I had been the one to blurt out the wrong truth at the wrong time. "No, I won't be wanting to stay here alone. I may be going back to the West Coast—I only came back to look after my mother, you know, when she had that first heart attack. I don't suppose I could afford the rent alone anyway."

"Well, that's another thing," he said. "You know this apartment was rent-controlled under the old law, and now the controls have been repealed, I was figuring on some—uh—some changes in the rent. Look, maybe we'd better talk about this some other time—"

"No." I tipped up the teacup and finished the second shot of Scotch. I felt warmer now. "There are too many ghosts here." He looked startled, but why should I explain? Father's old bathrobe hanging on the closet door, Mother's blue-and-white smock in the kitchen, Brad's room still full of the model airplanes of his teen years. No way I could spend the next months living with them. "When do you want me to move?"

"No hurry. Oh, no hurry." He muttered and apologized his way to the door, pausing on the threshold. "I brought up your mail, Sara. I'll leave it here."

When he had finally blundered his way out the door, I picked up the sheaf of envelopes. A week's accumulation. A windowed envelope from the telephone company. And now, there were other bills. No, I couldn't afford to keep this place now. I walked into my bedroom— there were fewer reminders here than anywhere else in the house; if I closed the door, perhaps, things would seem a bit more normal. I started to pour a third Scotch; then, resolutely, recapped the bottle; there seemed no particular point in getting drunk. And I wouldn't shut the door and pretend Mother and Father and Brad were still out there, either. That could lead to a quick trip to the local booby-hatch.

In one corner of the room, an easel was set up, with a half-finished watercolor on the board. Just before I'd come home to look after Mother, I'd gotten my second contract to illustrate a children's book—the first had given me a modest reputation when it won a small but prestigious award—and the illustrations were less than half finished. I had been dawdling along, since the publisher was not in a great hurry and I didn't greatly need the money; now I did. My father had had an adequate salary—but no life insurance except a modest burial policy. My mother's long illness had eaten up most of his slender savings. After the hospital and funeral expenses were paid, I estimated that I would have less than two hundred dollars in the bank. This would take me back to the West Coast, but it wouldn't give me enough to live on while finishing the book. Could I finish it, and get paid, before the lease was up here? And how many more unpaid bills would come to gobble up what little was left?

I opened the telephone bill and scowled at the total.

Through sheer inertia, I went on opening the stack of mail. Handwritten notes, mostly addressed to my father; probably condolences from acquaintances of my mother. A bill from Con Edison, and another from Macy's.

A letter addressed to me, with a Berkeley postmark. Roderick, I thought, and laid it aside. I would *not* let my present mood—sorrow, three drinks on an empty stomach, dark rain beating on the window—turn into lying to myself. I had never loved Roderick; I didn't love him now; our brief affair in Berkeley had been partly the workings of chemistry and propinquity, partly my own sexual curiosity. It had lasted almost four months; it had been fun; but even before Mother's heart attack called me back to New York, it was wearing thin. We had begun to lie to ourselves and each other; I had found myself too often exasperated by his grandiose plans for a year of study at the Sorbonne, his patronizing attitude to my own work—"You're a nice little book illustrator, but I somehow don't think you could make it in the real world of Art." *Even the sex hadn't been enough to smooth out the sudden, flaring quarrels; two or three times I'd found myself bored to death, suddenly demanding that he take me to bed because it seemed the easy way out of a dull evening, or a good way to ward off an endless wrangle about some trivial nothing. When our affair began, he had called me a witch—a green-eyed witch. All the Sara Latimers were witches—and anyhow, before we broke up he was making that "bitch" instead of "witch." Were the Sara Latimers all bitches too? Well, one of them died in childbirth in spite of no recorded marriage, and another had her name erased from the family Bible, so they must have been what my mother would have called "no better than they should have been." I'd never talked to Mother about Roderick. Even today girls don't usually talk to their mothers about the men they're sleeping with. It's the one bad aspect of the new sexual freedom; at least if you are married to the man you can be honest with your parents—they know you're sleeping with him and it gets taken for granted, which might be sort of nice.*

Oh, *damn* Roderick Hartmann anyhow! Unopened, I tossed his letter into the trash.

When he found I was leaving Berkeley, it had made him flare into passion again, and he'd asked me to marry him, probably flattering himself that I was going away in order to give myself time— or as they said in Berkeley, "space"—to get over our love affair. I hadn't told him the truth, and I felt flattered when he cried at the airport, putting me on the plane. Sara Latimer, bitch.

And now I was lonely, and I felt like I'd like to lie in his arms. (Or anybody's. Be honest, Sara; on a night like this, you'd go to bed with anybody halfway friendly and decent, just to forget the rain falling on those three graves. Don't con yourself into a situation like the one with Roderick again!)

Maybe I should call Mr. Patterson up for that drink again. *Stop it, Sara!* I admonished myself. *You are neither a witch or a bitch—yet!*

After Roderick's letter was a long, legal-sized envelope. The return address gave the address of a church. Something to do with the funeral? No; the postmark was, of all places, Arkham, Mass. Condolences from a distant relative? After all, our family tragedy had made headlines, and New York papers got into New England. (And what was it Father had said that day?—"You used to be related to half of New England.")

No, it was addressed to Paul Bradley Latimer, III—my father.

Faintly glad of any distraction, I tore it open. It was dated somewhat more than a week before, and read as follows:

Dear Sir:

A search by our legal advisors has determined that you are the owner (and sole heir at law) to the house on Witch Hill Road, formerly the property of Miss Sara Latimer, who was, I believe, your paternal aunt and who died a spinster seven years ago. The house has been standing vacant ever since, and although we have tried to keep it at least structurally sound, it may be in considerable disrepair by city standards, though in her last days Miss Latimer did have modern plumbing installed at her own expense, which was considerable.

After the death of Miss Latimer, I expressed interest in purchasing the house in behalf of our church's historical society. As you know, the house was built in 1645, and is one of the oldest houses which have not undergone extensive renovation, and still has the original foundations, in this part of the state. However, I was informed that until a search has been made for any other remaining heirs to the Latimer estate, the house and land could not be disposed of.

I am now in a position to make you a definite offer for the house and the property on which it stands. As I presume you do not wish to live here yourself, I would appreciate an early reply and a meeting to discuss the immediate transfer of the title of the property.

Yours truly,

Matthew Hay,
Pastor
Church of the Antique Rite

I read the letter twice, almost unable to comprehend. At the very moment where it seemed that I was penniless and without any resource of my own, suddenly I owned a house—even one in—what was the Reverend Mr. Hay's phrase?—"considerable disrepair by city standards." But after all, what did a rural pastor really know about city standards? Furthermore, there was a buyer for it, ready to make me a definite offer on behalf of their historical society. I had never heard of a church having a historical society before. For that matter, the Church of the Antique Rite was a new one on me, too. I wondered if it was a fundamentalist's revival movement, or whether it was one of the various nut-cult religions, like so many that had sprung up in Berkeley and elsewhere during the sixties, whose main tenet was pacifism, and whose major *raison d'être* was draft-dodging.

My father, who had raised the American flag on Guam after a bloody battle against Hirohito's suicide squads, would turn over in his grave—oh, God, how carelessly we use these clichés—at the idea of the family home falling into such hands.

Strange; I had never heard of my father's Aunt Sara until the day, the very hour, of his death—and now I owned her house. Resolution was growing in me. I had been cut off, by a sudden, vicious lightning-bolt of Fate, from all the family and all the security I had. Literally, after the first of the month, I wouldn't have a roof over my head.

So I would go to Arkham. I could live in the house, and finish my book there. The place was in disrepair—okay, if it was too bad, I could sell it, get an immediate advance of the money, and go somewhere else to finish my book. But I'd lived in student quarters in Berkeley, not to mention Roderick's studio, which he kept up, or rather *didn't* keep up, in the style of a hippie pad as he conceived such things to be. I could put up with primitive conditions—what was it that father said? *Aunt Sara didn't like electric lights?* Maybe she didn't like indoor plumbing either. I had heard that some of these back-country types didn't like the idea of having the toilet (thinking of it as an old-time privy) inside the house next to the kitchen. Oh, well, I could put up with that too, for a couple of months.

It was a place to go. And perhaps, if there was a local historical society, the Reverend Mr. Hay could tell me something of my family—finish the story which had been cruelly cut short by my father's death.

I did not recognize, then, the reason for my own sudden eagerness to have a place again, roots, a family history. I just knew that suddenly there was a place to go; from having no plans, no home, no future, I could think ahead again.

I went to the window, carefully removing the half-finished watercolor—thank goodness it was dry—and began dismantling the easel, ready to fold it and pack it away first thing in the morning.

TWO

HAUNTED INHERITANCE

THE JOURNEY TO ARKHAM WAS MORE COMPLEX THAN I COULD have believed. I'd lived in New York or Berkeley all my life and I'd grown accustomed to being able to board a plane or train for any part of the known universe at a moment's notice.

This one wasn't like that. To get to Arkham I had to take a train to Providence, Rhode Island, get a bus from there to Wareham, Massachusetts, then wait for the small, suburban bus which wound northward along the Massachusetts coast, stopping at every hamlet and wide spot in the road, until finally, late in the day, it could disgorge me in Arkham . . . and from there, probably, a mile or two by taxi to Witch Hill itself.

I'd have preferred to arrive early in the afternoon; the bus company told me, indifferently, that the bus which arrived at 6:00 P.M. was all the bus there was, implying, though they didn't say, that if I didn't like it, I'd have to do the next best thing—and I wasn't even sure what that might be.

Since the only alternative would have been to rent a car, and inquiries quickly convinced me that this would drain my slender resources to the breaking point, I took the train to Providence and the bus to Massachusetts, then bought the ticket for Arkham, inquiring how to get from there to the hamlet of Witch Hill. They didn't know, and, I assumed, couldn't have cared less; it wasn't on their route.

When I insisted, they dragged out a local road map and after a reasonably careful study, informed me that there wasn't any such place.

I shrugged and hoisted my two suitcases and the portfolio with my easel and paints on to the Arkham bus anyhow. I remembered reading, once, that there were over ten thousand unincorporated towns and villages in the United States which didn't appear on any map. Obviously, the house existed *somewhere*—I had an offer to buy it tucked away in my purse. Someone in Arkham was certain to know where the place was. If all else failed, I could spend the night at a hotel, and tomorrow morning consult the Post Office. If my great-aunt Sara had ever received any letters—and in this day and age, everybody did, even if it was only the yearly form 1040 from an otherwise indifferent government—the Post Office would know where they'd been delivered.

The Arkham bus betrayed, by its rusty blue and white paint and general air of decrepitude, that even Arkham was very far from being a center of civilization. Only half a dozen of the frayed leather seats were occupied, by shabbily dressed back-country types who stared with overt curiosity at my bright-red canvas luggage and running shoes. The few women I saw from the bus window seemed to be elderly, wearing flowered house dresses well below their knees, and loose baggy sweaters, or foreign, in rusty-looking black skirts and dark coats. After a few miles the bus left the paved road and took a loopy, curving track along narrow dirt roads which wound through the hills and wooded slopes, passing isolated, dead-looking farms and tumbledown villages. Every twenty minutes or so it would pull up at a crossroads with a cluster of mailboxes, or stop briefly before an old, steepled, and belfried church with flaking grey or white paint, or a little country store showing everything from chicken feed to kerosene lamps in the window, and a couple of lonesome gas pumps, their bright and familiar signs—Exxon, Gulf, Shell—the only visible link to the metropolis behind me. It took on, or let off, a small handful of passengers here and there, mostly old people or schoolchildren. Most of them appeared to be known to the driver, who chatted with them in low tones or asked about absent members of the family.

Late in the day, after hours of winding along the roads and through the hills, the dirt road gave way again to a clumsily paved narrow highway, which in turn evolved into a cobbled street, and the bus began to climb up into the steep, hilly streets of old Arkham. It wound through suburbs of old New England mansions, now mostly cut up for rooming houses, passed the wide-flung lawns and heavy, ivy-hung brick and stone buildings of a college campus—I saw a sign informing me that this was Miskatonic University, and realized that I'd never heard of the place.

Evidently neither their academic record nor their football team had ever put them on the map. Anyway, it seemed unlikely that any Space Age professors of more than local reputation could be lured out here when there were hosts of big, modern, and even accessible campuses to draw away the better students—even, if they were hardy New Englanders—to Boston with its Harvard and M.I.T., or to Providence and its Brown University. I supposed Miskatonic was one of those small, inexpensive local colleges which turn the upwardly-mobile sons and daughters of the local farmers and shopkeepers into schoolteachers, librarians, educated farmers, and certified public accountants.

Just the same, it was a picturesque old campus, with its bell-tower and steep-sided stone church, and I found myself wondering if the Art Department was worth investigating. It was, at least, accessible from where I lived, and I didn't feel that I wanted to be entirely cut off from any sort of intellectual life out here, even for three months.

The sun was slanting low, even for the lengthening late-spring day, when I disembarked at the Arkham bus station. After a hasty but surprisingly good light supper in the small restaurant there—chicken pie considerably fresher than the frozen ones I could buy in the city—I inquired around and discovered that the town of Witch Hill (population, the bus clerk told me, about seventy-five) could be reached by a bus which theoretically connected with the bus I had just left, was leaving right about now, and would arrive at Witch Hill post office in forty-five minutes. And how far away was it? Oh, only about eleven miles, something like that, but those roads back there in the hills were pretty bad. Could I get a taxi there to take me to my house?

Well, she didn't know about a taxi, but if the house was in the village I could walk to any house there within five minutes or so.

"You do know, it's a *real small* town," she informed me—I could have guessed that by now, and if it was small by Arkham standards, it must *really* be small by New York ones—and it was with a certain amount of misgiving that I boarded the bus. I was actually thinking that I should stay in Arkham overnight, and try to get a taxi or a rented car out there by daylight. But I had boarded the New Haven train that morning at ten, and I was stiff and tired with the long ride. I wanted the trip to be over!

The bus which I now boarded made the Arkham bus look new and streamlined; I had seen buses like this in museums and in old silent films on the Late Late Show. Over the door was a hand-printed sign reading ARKHAM-INNSMOUTH. There were only two passengers other than myself, one a loutish youth with a vacant stare suggesting that the local equivalent of the Jukes and the Kallikaks played some part in his ancestry (to my immense relief he disembarked at the first stop), the other an old and very fat man who carried two lobster pots under his arm and whose clothing and person exhaled a pronounced, but wholesome, smell of fish.

After he, too, had disembarked at a lonesome crossroads where a winding path led down to a cluster of grey shacks and a gleam of distant ocean, the bus driver, who was old and fatherly, asked me:

"How far are you going, Miss?"

I told him, and he said, "Is there someone to meet you, Miss? Witch Hill Road is almost half a mile from town, it's way out in the country. You don't live there, do you? I know almost everybody along this road."

I moved into the front seat where I could talk to him. "I've never been here," I said. "My family lived here for generations, though I believe they're all dead now. Do you know them? My name is Latimer."

"Latimer, Latimer—no, I never knew any of the family," the driver said. "I've only been on this bus route six months or so. I heard people speak of the old Latimer house out on Witch Hill Road somewhere, but I understood there was only an old lady living alone there, years ago, and since she died the house's been deserted. She's been dead for years. That can't be your folks, Miss!"

"I'm afraid it is, though. I just inherited the house."

He twisted in his seat and looked shocked. "Look here, Miss, you can't drag all your luggage half a mile down that road after dark. The Witch Hill Road stop is just a mailbox! You'd better go into Madison Corners with the bus, and try to get someone to drive you out there."

"And suppose I can't? Then I'll be a whole mile away from the house, won't I?"

"Then you can wait in the store there till I come back from Innsmouth, and I'll drive you out there myself," he said. "I reach Innsmouth about nine-thirty, and come back through here on the way back to Arkham at eleven. Or you could go in to Arkham and come out by daylight. But I reckon somebody there can drive you. Jeb Meyers hangs around the store with his farm truck most of the time, picking up an odd buck now and then to drive people home in the rain or if they've got heavy stuff to lug, and he's sure to be there waiting for the bus."

As he spoke, he slowed for an isolated red light, winking like a flashing eye before a small cluster of buildings; a country store, a small post office, a gas station, and two or three other buildings. "Madison Corners, Miss Latimer, and there's Jeb's farm truck over there. Let me help you with that suitcase. Well, I hope you find your house all right, and remember, I go past the Witch Hill stop toward Arkham twice a day; ten-thirty in the morning and eleven at night. Anytime you want to go into Arkham you can get the bus out there, no need to come into the Corners."

"And suppose I want to go to Innsmouth? What time do you pass to Innsmouth?" I asked. He frowned and kindly shook his head. "You don't want to go to Innsmouth, Miss. There ain't *nobody* wants to go to Innsmouth."

I clambered down and watched the empty bus drive away. I felt forlorn, as if I had lost the last contact with any friendly face; but then I realized that already it was growing dark—the driver of the bus had already switched on his lights—and that an ominous rumble in the sky proclaimed oncoming rain and one of the swift harsh coastal storms. I walked firmly over to the dusty rattletrap farm truck parked outside the country store.

"Are you Jeb Meyers?" I asked. "The bus driver told me I could get a ride with you out to Witch Hill Road."

The old man behind the wheel of the truck nodded his grey head slowly.

He was an unprepossessing specimen, coarse-featured, with eyes half-hidden behind steel-rimmed glasses, and a stubble of coarse beard, but I told myself that I couldn't expect Fifth Avenue grooming in Madison Corners. He said, in the harsh New England twang I had come to expect, "Ayeh, my name's Meyers. Reckon I can give you a ride. Cost you a buck, and fifty cents if you got a trunk to handle. Where at you want to go?"

He hardly sounded cordial, but compared to the average Brooklyn taxi driver, he was almost effusive. I said, "I'm not sure where the house is. Probably you know it. There's no street address, but it's on Witch Hill Road, and the name is Latimer."

"You don't want to go there, Miss," he said. "The folks there are all dead."

I began to wonder if the man was, as my father would have said, not playing with a full deck.

"I'm aware of that," I said. "I own the house now. My name is Sara Latimer."

For the first time he raised his eyes and really looked at me. His mouth fell open, giving him a pop-eyed look. He blinked, and I saw his oversized Adam's apple bob up and down once or twice.

"So you did come back," he said. "You did come back like they said you would. You're *not* dead, Miss?"

Oh, God! Talk about asking a silly question—I debated answering *Yes, of course I am, they just forgot to bury me,* but the ill-timed jest stuck in my throat. Besides, if he were really that stupid, he'd take me literally.

"What on earth is the matter with you? Of course I'm not dead—I never have been, as far as I know," I said crisply. "I take it you *do* know where the Latimer house is?"

"Yep. Yep. You know I do, Ma'am—Miss Sara. You forgot how often I used to deliver your groceries and all like that? No offense, Miss." He swiveled his head to stare at me while he twisted the door handle and hauled out his overalled figure. He never took his eyes off me. What in the world was wrong with the man? Had he never seen a woman's legs? Maybe this part of the world wasn't the right place to wear jeans. Since my great-aunt Sara had been, at the very least, upwards of sixty when she died—no, more likely eighty; my father had been sixty-two and she'd been part of *his* father's generation—he could hardly mistake me for *her* alive or dead!

Or was he senile, and remembering her at my age? Was there some sort of family resemblance? Be that as it may, it seemed that my transit problems were solved, at least, and if he delivered groceries to the house as well, that was another problem out of the way.

The small grocery store was still lighted, and a few farmers lingered inside by the counters. I said, "I want to go inside and get a couple of things for tomorrow. Can you put my suitcases inside your truck and wait a minute or two?"

"Sure can," he said, complying, "but no one round here's likely to steal nothing. Most folks don't even own no keys to their doors."

It wasn't a thought calculated to add to my peace of mind just now, but I passed it off and went into the store. It was a kind I believed had vanished from the face of the earth, perhaps the remote ancestor of those California drug stores where you can get anything from auto tires to caviar; in this little country store, besides the usual assortment of groceries packaged and tinned, I saw snow shovels, dog collars, lampshades, children's blue jeans, socks and underwear, knitting yarn, fish lines, spark plugs, sandals, hot-water bottles, and kerosene, as well as a number of articles too strange to identify or enumerate. I bought a loaf of bread, half a pound of butter, a dozen eggs, a pound of bacon, a box of teabags, two quarts of milk, and, remembering at the last minute my great-aunt Sara's prejudice against electric light, a flashlight as well.

"You'd better buy batteries for that, too," observed a lean, smiling young man who was standing at the counter as I picked up the flashlight.

I flushed, picking up an assortment of batteries. "Thank you. I can't imagine where my head's at! There are no electric lights in the house, and if I wake up in the night—"

"Good lord," he said. "You'd better get kerosene, too. There are sure to be lamps, but you can never be sure of the oil supply!"

I confessed, "I've never even seen a kerosene lamp!"

"No," he said, moving to my side, "you don't look like a local product." He looked down and smiled, and I felt a little shock of electric warmth.

It was the first time since the sudden shattering deaths that I had heard a human voice addressed directly to me, seen a friendly, intimate smile. To my sense of isolation and defensiveness it was like the sun suddenly coming out. I almost sighed with relief, and held out my hand.

"I'm new to the neighborhood," I said. "My great-aunt died several years ago, and I'm coming to stay in the family house for the summer. My name's Sara Latimer."

Behind me, at the counter where my modest groceries were being packed, I heard a sharp, drawn breath. I didn't care; my eyes were on the young man. He smiled, quickly and warmly, again. He said, "Of course; I know the house. It's a bit of a landmark, I believe; but it's been closed up for years. I'm Brian Standish." He took my extended hand in his, briefly. His hands were large, the fingers soft and well-manicured, but they looked strong and competent.

"I'm here to help my—I guess I'd have to say cousin—really he's one of those New England distant relatives that nobody can ever figure out just what the relationship is; my great-aunt's stepson's sister's husband, or something like that—with his practice; I just finished up my internship at Johns Hopkins, and I thought I'd like a summer in the country before I went back as a resident." *Of course,* I thought, *those fine hands had to belong to either an artist or a doctor.*

Brian Standish had brown curly hair, which came down in long sideburns around his tanned cheeks, and his eyes were brown and twinkling. "Where are you here from? New York City? Oh, good grief, you can't walk into an old farmhouse after dark all alone, not even knowing how to light a kerosene lamp!"

"I don't think I have much choice," I said. "What's the alternative? I haven't seen any hotels around here, even if I could afford one.

And if I went back to Arkham, it would simply mean coming back tomorrow."

He frowned. "If I were at home, I'd take you to my mother and offer you a bed for the night," he said. "If in my own house I would anyway—all very nice and above board, I have a nice big sofa, and you could have my bed. But I'm afraid Cousin James wouldn't understand. This isn't New York, after all." I was beginning to get that idea. After a minute I said, "Well, yes, I sort of guessed that. It's very nice of you, but—"

"The alternative, I guess," he went on as if he had not heard me, "is for you to hop in my car and I'll drive you out there, light the lamps for you, and make sure you're going to be all right."

I hesitated only a moment. I hadn't realized they made that kind of man any more. "Thanks a lot, I'd appreciate that more than you can imagine, Dr. Standish."

"Brian—"

"Brian, then. My bags are out there—"

"Yes, I saw you talking to old Jeb. He's one of the local characters—I ought to warn you to take anything he says not with a grain but a whole shaker-full of salt. Oh, I guess you'd be safe enough with the old fellow, but he just isn't very bright and he'd think nothing of dropping you off there to fend for yourself the way a farm girl would."

Brian Standish waited while I paid for my groceries and the can of kerosene, tucked them under his long arm, and strode out to the waiting truck. "I'm going to drive Miss Latimer home, Jeb," he said. "Hand me out her bags, if you will."

Jeb looked sullen, obviously disgruntled at the loss of a fare; Brian handed him a dollar bill, at which he glowered a little less, and he turned over my bags, still muttering and glancing sidewise at me. I heard him say, "So it's started already," but paid no attention. Old Jeb may not have been the village idiot—he must have been intelli-

gent enough to get a driver's license—but he certainly wasn't all that
far from it. I followed Brian to a small and rather dusty VW and
waited while he stowed my bags inside and wrestled with the portfolio and folding easel. "I guess the trunk won't hold it; can you
manage it on your lap," he asked, "or shall I have Jeb bring it up in
the truck tomorrow? What is it, anyway?"

I told him, stowing myself into the seat with the easel canted up
sidewise and partly blocking my view of the road. He raised his
brows in interest. "You're an artist?"

"I illustrate children's books," I told him. "There is a small, but
distinct difference, or so I've always been told." Oddly, the memory
of Roderick's put-down now held no pain, maybe because Dr. Standish looked impressed. He got in beside me and started the car, and
simultaneously a clap of thunder crashed across the sky and a sudden
harsh spatter of rain set the windshield awash.

"Lucky I picked you up," he chuckled, "that farm truck of Jeb's
leaks—not to mention that the old fellow's top speed is twenty miles
an hour on the highway."

I laughed back: "Considering the way he talks, I'd feel safer with
him at twenty than at fifty!"

"There *is* that," he agreed. He put the car in gear, and slowly
backed, turned, and slid away from the lighted buildings. A couple
of minutes later, he turned into the Witch Hill Road, then had to
halt and shift the car into second gear to ease it up the rutted, already
rain-slick mud road. A sudden flare of lightning half blinded me, and
Brian swore under his breath, fighting the wheel.

"I'm putting you to an awful lot of trouble—" I said apologeti-
cally.

"Think nothing of it. If I'm going to have a country practice—
and I am, sooner or later—I'll just have to get used to driving out in
all kinds of weather, all kinds of roads, all hours of the day and
night," Brian said cheerfully. "And I learned to cope with a kerosene

lamp years ago; I grew up in a town like this, and out here, every third rainstorm knocks the power lines down, and it's back to lamps and candles anyhow. Your Aunt Sara had the right idea—one less thing to go out of order!"

"Did you know her—my Aunt Sara?"

"No, not really. No; only by reputation as a crotchety old dame, definitely one of the local characters. I may have seen her a time or two before I went away to medical school. The fact is—" he hesitated, then asked, "Did *you* know her?"

"I never even heard of her until last week," I confessed. "From what my father said before she died, I gather she was—eccentric."

"To say the least," Brian agreed. "Of course, the local population is like the Dark Ages, you know. We don't get TV back here, even Arkham is a fringe area, and the hills make it hard even to get radio. When the Moon walk took place a few years ago, I doubt if anyone in town even knew about it, and when it was in the papers, one man summed up the local attitude very well—he just said you couldn't believe all that stuff you got out of Washington.

"Since you never knew your late lamented aunt, you won't be too offended to learn that she was locally regarded as a witch, or something like that."

"Family tradition," I said ruefully. "I understand that another of our ancestresses was hanged as a witch about three hundred years ago."

"Arkham had plenty of them," Brian said. Abruptly, slowing the car, he said, "There it is—the Latimer house."

A deafening clap of thunder drowned his words, and by a sudden flare of lightning I saw it, for the first time, stark against the sky—revealed in all the insane ugliness of turret, balcony, gaping black windows, porches like jagged teeth. The lightning winked out, leaving me wondering if I had really seen it at all or if it could possibly look like that.

"I don't believe it," I said weakly, "there ain't, as the old farmer said about the giraffe, no such animal. Is that a *house,* or a set for a Frankenstein movie?"

Brian laughed, softly and sympathetically. I felt his hand leave the wheel and gently slide over mine. "I thought I'd better not leave it to old Jeb to pick you up off the floor when you got your first sight of it."

"Whoever built a house like *that,*" I said, "ought to have to haunt it. Heavens preserve us, I don't *believe* it. I hope it's better inside than out."

"Bound to be," said Brian. "Couldn't be worse."

Now I could see it in the headlights of the car. It was worse than it had looked by the lightning, because I could no longer avoid any hideous detail. I wondered even at that how much the dimness of the lights softened it. Oh, well. I'd wait till daylight—I'd be *happy* to wait till daylight for a good look at the monstrosity. "It might be perfectly comfortable inside," I said, whistling in the dark. "After all, God-knows-how-many generations of my family not only lived there, but presumably *chose* to live there, and prospered after a fashion."

"I'll pull right up under the *porte-cochère,* and we won't get wet; it's got one good feature right away," Brian said. "Have you the keys?"

I did. A call to the family lawyer in Providence had provided me with keys, and with the information that the house was fully furnished, which had prompted me to sell some of the furniture from the apartment and put the rest in storage. I carried the groceries to the door and fumbled with the keys while Brian brought my bags over. The door creaked, groaned with a shrieking of well-rusted hinges, and finally yielded. Brian said, "You'd better have that flashlight—wait till I get the batteries in it. Here." A thin bright ray of light shone through the darkness, guiding me over the steps.

I stood in a huge, shadowy cavern of damp-smelling space, enormous dark shapes of furniture around me. The room was fitfully lit by the recurrent lightning. I took the flashlight for a moment from Brian; trained it around the room, taking in briefly the huge old carved chairs and horsehair sofa, the vast cavern of fireplace, the mantel above it. I brought the flashlight beam to rest on an enormous painting above the mantel, and gasped—

I looked into my own face.

THREE

SARA THE FIRST

IN THE SHOCK OF THAT MOMENT THE FLASHLIGHT DROPPED, bounced, and skittered across the floor. I think I cried out in shock. Then Brian's arm, warm and reassuring, was around my shoulders.

"Take it easy, Sara, I'm here. What's the matter? What frightened you? It's only a painting." He bent to recover the flashlight; trained it upwards again. "But what a resemblance! I presume that's the ancestress?" He went on talking, gently, to reassure me, while my breathing quieted to normal. "If so, it was painted in her prime; she's a beauty. The one or two times I saw her, of course, she was an old, old woman and it was easy to believe that she was a witch. But the original witches were supposed to be real glamour girls, weren't they? Isn't that where the word *glamour* originally came from? Look, Sara, it's like looking in a mirror."

Slowly I recovered my poise and presence of mind. It had been silly to cry out, to lose my composure, but the surprise of coming into a totally strange house, into a dark, unfamiliar, lightning-lit room, and seeing myself there, very much a part of this strange house—it was a shock I couldn't have allowed for at all. I raised my eyes again and studied the painting.

It was, indeed, very much like looking into a mirror. The woman in the painting was tall, slight, full-figured—a bit more so than I— and wore the typical Victorian high-necked shirtwaist, ruffled at the neck with white. But the face was my own, pointed into a slender triangle of wide forehead and narrow chin, with straight dark eyebrows, wide green eyes—Roderick had said they made me look like a cat— and loose, wavy red-blonde hair. The coloring was unusual enough that I'd long since given up trying to wear makeup—I just looked painted. It occurred to me that if Father had grown up in a house with this painting in the hall, he must have been reminded, every day, that one of the ill-fated Sara Latimers had, indeed, been born into his family. Yet he had never spoken of it until the shock of the family tragedy had broken down his reticence. A mystery indeed!

Well, at least this explained old Jeb Meyers's reaction.

I wrenched my eyes away from the portrait, coming back to the awareness that Brian's arm was still solicitously around me. A little reluctantly—how warm and comforting it felt!—I drew away from him. I said, "I suppose we'd better start looking for those lamps and get them lighted."

Was it my imagination or did he sound regretful too? "I suppose so. Let me think; they'll probably be back in the kitchen, if we can find it."

Guided by the wavering light of the flashlight, we explored the dark doors leading off the old parlor. We went through a dim hallway, flashed the light briefly into a dusty, book-lined room, looked inside to what appeared to be, to my intense relief, a bathroom; huge, spindly-legged iron tub, high basin with ornate Victorian faucets, discreetly enclosed antique toilet with an old-fashioned overhead tank and pull-chain. Comfortless and ugly as it was, at least I need not brave thunderstorms, spiders and unknown country beasties in search of the old outhouse!

The next room was the kitchen, and a brief search of the old chintz-covered shelves revealed a pair of glass kerosene lamps; I held the flashlight while Brian filled, pumped, and lighted, and within ten minutes soft bright light was illuminating every nook and corner of the old high-ceilinged room, with its paneled, blue-painted dado and old-fashioned flowered wallpaper. There was dust aplenty—after all, I thought, the place has been shut up for seven years—but it was cleaner than I expected and looked comfortable enough.

"Cheers," Brian said, "I was afraid it would be a coal range and you'd be stuck with cold food until someone could arrange a load of coal. But there's a gas range; let's see if it's all turned off, or if they left it connected up. In these isolated houses, they usually cook with bottled gas anyway, and there's likely to be part of a tank left. Unless it's rusted shut; and propane tanks don't usually do that too easily."

He experimented with matches, and discovered that, once the dust was brushed away, a pale blue flame leaped forth. "You'll have to order more in a day or two," he said, "but this will let you make coffee—or tea or whatever—and cook yourself a couple of scratch meals."

He glanced half-heartedly at the door. "I suppose, if and when the rain lets up a little, I ought to be on my way. I've gotten a lamp lighted, and I don't suppose I ought to use that as an excuse to hang around."

"Oh, no!" It was an instantaneous protest, which I amended, half ashamed. "I'm sorry; I know you're a doctor, and if you have a patient waiting, I know I mustn't keep you. Only, if you haven't—I wish you'd stay and at least go through the place once with me. I feel like a ninny to be scared—I mean, it's been my family home for I forget how many generations, but still—"

"If that's the way you feel, you can't get rid of me," he said firmly. "It's Cousin James's night to handle any calls that come in—and I've always wanted to explore a haunted house after dark!"

I found myself shivering. "I know you're joking—but don't. I've got to *live* here! I'm not superstitious—or at least I never thought I was—but then I never saw a house like this."

He put his arm around my waist. "Well, if it's haunted—it's haunted by your own great-aunt, and she's enough like you that she certainly wouldn't hurt her own double!"

I wasn't so sure. Father had evidently thought of her as an unholy terror. But I didn't say so.

The soft, full light of the kerosene lamp dispelled the shadows in the big kitchen; I decided to leave the groceries in their bag until I could scrub a shelf or two clean. Also I made a mental note to see about ice deliveries. Lamp in hand, Brian and I went back through the big living room. Now that I could see the painting clearly, the resemblance was even more striking, and for a moment I had the curious illusion that the painted face, so like my own, winked down at me.

So there you are, my girl, after all those years. Sara Latimer—another Sara Latimer. Your father couldn't keep you from becoming one of us.

"Rubbish, my dear aunt," I said aloud, and turned back to Brian. "Let's explore the rest of the house."

As we went through the maze of the small back rooms—pantries, a screened sunporch, a large room that Brian said was a summer kitchen, closets, bedrooms sparsely furnished with narrow beds and rickety bureaus, which he said were maid's rooms and which looked as if no one had slept in them since the turn of the century—I found myself telling Brian of the circumstances which had brought me here. When I spoke of the deaths I could not keep my voice quite steady. Sympathy would have broken me up, but he simply squeezed my hand for a moment and said, "You've been hit pretty hard. Maybe this is what you need—a nice, quiet place, work to do, and some new friends."

A narrow and eminently breakneck staircase angled upward from the back kitchen, but Brian vetoed climbing it. "I know old houses. The front staircase will be in better repair."

We retraced our steps through the front of the house and started upward. The light of the lamp, borne aloft in Brian's hand, cast weird shadows over the banisters, elongating them into monstrous black forms that seemed to march along the staircase with us. At the curve of the staircase a second portrait of Sara Latimer regarded us with a level, baleful gaze.

"Sara the First believes in keeping an eye on things," I said, trying to sound flippant. *Only, of course, she was about Sara the twelfth, or thereabouts. I hope they don't all haunt this place!*

Three of the second-floor rooms were empty, or tenanted only by trunks or shadowy boxes, great antique furniture shoved into corners. For the first time I found it credible that Sara Latimer my ancestress had lived here alone for many years, and that the house had been shut up, untenanted, for seven years since her death.

"The place is an antique dealer's paradise," said Brian. "You can have a ball exploring it by daylight and finding all the family treasures. Promise you'll let me come and help you rummage through all these fascinating trunks and boxes!"

"I'll be glad of all the help I can get, believe me."

Secretly I wondered if the memory of this place was the reason for my father's inordinate hatred of antique or Victorian furniture. Our home had been furnished with the newest and best of Swedish modern, and I had put it all in storage. Maybe I could sell some of this stuff off to antique dealers to pay for storage of the rest.

I pushed the fourth door. Immediately I realized; this was the heart of the house, this was Aunt Sara's personal domain.

As the door opened, a strange, sweet smell, curiously pungent, drifted into the hallway. The lamplight showed me that this room was fully furnished, dominated by an enormous four-poster bed. It must have been king-size or better, and was covered and draped by a huge white curtained canopy.

Brian stared and the light dipped. He said, sounding awed, "And to think I had the nerve to offer you a bed for the night, with *that* waiting for you!"

I gulped. "It's enormous, isn't it? All that just for one little old lady! I wonder if she really spent every night of her life alone in it!"

"I wouldn't know," Brian said. "She died and was buried as a spinster, but if she was really as beautiful as those portraits, I'd bet heavy odds she had company *some* of those nights at least."

I felt faintly abashed. Brian and I were not really on terms to be discussing beds, and yet, since we had come into this room, so overwhelmingly dominated by the great four-poster, we had been looking at nothing else.

I said, "It makes me think of those primary French lessons. The pencil of my grandfather. The bed of my great-aunt."

"The bed of your great-aunt is *formidable*," Brian said with an uneasy laugh. "I hate to think of you sleeping all alone in it—." He stopped, abruptly, and by lamplight I could see that his ears were faintly red. "I'm sorry, Sara, I've no idea what got into me, I didn't mean that the way it sounded."

"You'd better call me Sally. Sara Latimer is so *absolutely* the old hag out there." Secretly I made up mind that my first move tomorrow would be to take down my great-aunt's portrait. I might bring myself to live in her house, but I wasn't going to spend my whole damn summer under her green eyes!

"But Sally doesn't suit you. You *look* like a Sara," he protested, "and she isn't an old hag—at least not in those portraits; she's almost as beautiful as you are!"

I went over to the bed. It was covered with an ancient and beautiful coverlet in an elaborate patchwork design with a motif of five-pointed stars. I drew it back, feeling the sheets. They were immaculately clean, although somewhat damp.

Brian pointed to the corner of the room, where a huge clothespress stood, great and dismal as a funeral vault. He said, "If memory serves me rightly, that big dark thingy there is an airing-closet, for

storing linens. You would probably find fresh ones in there. Sleeping
in damp sheets is what used to give old New Englanders rheumatism."

Inside the closet there were stacks of fresh sheets, all smooth linen,
as dry and fresh as if Aunt Sara had stacked them there only yesterday
instead of seven years ago; Brian set the lamp on a huge high bureau
and together we stripped and made the bed.

"Brian, be a dear and fetch my small overnight case upstairs," I
said. "I draw the line at sleeping in one of Aunt Sara's nighties."

While he foraged with the flashlight for the case, I looked around
the room further by lamplight. There was a small marble sink in the
corner, with ornamental bronze taps, where I could brush my teeth
without going downstairs, if I chose. An enormous wavering mirror
over it gave me back my own face, my still windblown hair puffed
loose until it looked uncannily like Sara the First's. *Damn* Sara the
First! If she'd been the witch my father said, she was probably already
well damned without any interference from me.

In the corner was a huge dressing table, high on ornately carved
legs, marble-topped, with an old-fashioned ivory-backed comb, brush,
and hand mirror. I sat down for a moment on the low bench, looking
into the big, wavering, tilted mirror above, picking up the hand mirror. *For such an old lady, Aunt Sara had had a passion for mirrors.* Scattered
on the vast marble top were small bottles and jars. Many of them were
silver-topped or cut glass, all very beautiful and quite expensive. The
image in the mirror wavered, and for a moment it seemed that Aunt
Sara's painted face looked out at me. The lips were moist, red, and
parted; the hair sensuously tumbling, long around the shoulders; the
eyes gleamed green, and the shoulders were bare above small, hard,
pointed breasts—

I raised my head at Brian's footsteps; he set the overnight case
down beside me, and came and stood behind me, his hands on my
shoulders, his face looming close over mine in the mirror, and for a moment it seemed that his face, too, flowed and twisted, until it seemed
that a naked man stood there—I wrenched my eyes away from the il-

lusion, flushing. What would Aunt Sara think about a man in her old-maid bedroom? Probably she was the sort who always looked for a man under the bed before she climbed into her four-poster.

"What are all the little bottles and jars?" Brian asked. "The whole room smells of herbs; is that smell lavender?"

I shook my head. "Not lavender, no. My mother used to use lavender sachet; I know that smell. I don't know what it is." It was somehow dizzying. I untwisted the silver cap of a small porcelain pot. "Chances are this stuff is Lydia Pinkham's Cold Cream, or some such."

"It isn't," Brian said soberly. "She evidently went in for making her own herbal cosmetics—a lot of people around here still swear by herbal medicines, and herb teas, and the strange thing is, they get well. There's a lot in folk medicine, if someone could explore it— what *is* that smell?"

From the opened top of the porcelain jar, a strong, sweet, almost dizzying odor rushed out, almost a visible cloud of fragrance that seemed to spread and fill the entire room. I breathed it in; and it seemed to ascend to my head like a strong drink, making me dizzy. A whirling cloud of fantasies, erotic visions, strong sensations, engulfed me.

Brian bent over me to breathe it more deeply. He drew it in, then leaned over, tilted my head back and kissed me on the lips. His mouth felt hot and hard, and he thrust his body against my back. His hands searched for my breasts.

As if compelled, I reached my finger into the porcelain jar, dabbed a trace of the sweet scented cream on the thin skin at the base of my throat; pushed the jar away, twisting it shut again. Brian came around to me, kneeling to push his face against my breasts, his hands pulling buttons apart on my blouse.

In the dizzying, scented lamplight, I had the strange sense that I was moving under deep waters. I stood up, gently loosening Brian's hands; as if in a trance, I flung off my clothes. In the wavering light on the old mirror I saw my own nakedness, tall and thin and pale, my hair a bright spot, my mouth hot and red like a glistening rose, the blotch of red-brown body hair above my groin. Neither Brian nor I spoke; as if hypnotized, his own hands moved on shirt buttons; he shrugged away the shirt, slid down the zipper, kicked away his trousers. He was dark and hairy, and already hard and erect as he came toward me, his dark eyes gleaming and glowing with a reddish light in the lamplight.

He bent over me with a soft laugh, his mouth closing over mine; with a wild laugh of exultation, I flung my arms around him, and my teeth closed in his lip; I felt the salt taste of blood in my mouth.

His strong arms swung me free of the floor; then he bore me down and back on the scented sheets, and I sank; sinking into the scent as my body sank under his into the soft featherbed. Above me, in the lamplight, the swaying canopy danced. A thunderclap, and a wild spatter of rain slashing on the window, drowned my wordless cry as he came into me, savagely hard, wildly intense, his lips covering mine, squashing me back into the pillows.

Surrendering myself without thought to the wildness of the moment, I felt my body moving, thrashing with unaccustomed response. Against the light his naked body seemed to grow and swell, to waver and go deliriously out of focus until he loomed above me with demoniac hugeness, pounding, battering, growing and shrinking like some devil-figure, now human, now savage beast. There was none of the tenderness I had always desired before. There was nothing gentle, or romantic. It was a wild, frantic, almost animal coupling, going on and on and on until I thought I should explode in the frenzy of it, and wild thoughts spun in my head . . . *back, back from the darkness . . . Asmodeus, Azanoor, dark above me . . . my body to the beast and my soul to hell* . . . with the frantic writhing of my own hips, the incessant drumming beat of his movements . . . then I heard his savage shout of exultation and my own scream of mindless delight, mingling with it and drowning out the final roll of thunder.

We rolled wordlessly apart and slept like the dead.

I dreamed. I dreamed I was standing on a vast, barren plain, covered with low weird tumuli, asymmetric and strange, with a curious grey light all round me and odd beasts moving in the distance; but I felt no fear. I was naked, and moved without volition over the ground, which was covered with twisted, knotted, colorless grass, and strewn with low mounds and fallen stones. The eerie light brightened a little, and I could see now that the stones were gravestones. I noted, without curiosity, that one of them read SARA MAGDALEN LATIMER: Savaged here to death by dogs, 1884. *And the dogs did eat her flesh . . . Kings . . .* the number of chapter and verse were illegible.

I moved past the other gravestones, seeing with an equal lack of curiosity the names of other Sara Latimers and the violent deaths they had met. The curious unearthly light was like no moonlight or sunlight I had ever seen. As I floated on in the curious astral light, I felt, rather than saw, a shadow, which loomed higher and higher as I came near. A voice was calling in the distance:

"Sara! Sara!"

The shadow rose higher; higher. I saw that it was a blasted oak tree, stark against the sky, and as I floated to its foot, I saw the inscription with curious, burnt-fire letters;

Sara Latimer she was y-hanged on thicce oake as a wytch on ye 31 August 1671 and may ye soule of her rest damned through all eternytie.

I thought with a fragment of awareness, really, how naive.

A thunderclap rocked the sky; a great lightning-bolt split the oak, which toppled, weird slow-motion, toward me—and I woke with a gasp and a cry, to hear Brian softly murmuring my name.

"Sara—Sara?"

I found myself blushing in the dark. Good God, what had *happened* to me? My family hadn't been dead a week, and here I was, rutting like a bitch in bed with a perfect stranger, a man I'd met less than four hours ago—

"Brian? I was asleep."

"I know, love, and I hate to waken you, but you were moaning in your sleep, and I was afraid you were having a nightmare."

"I know; I was dreaming of all the Sara Latimers. They all met with violent deaths, you know—"

He bent down and kissed me. "Don't be morbid, sweetheart; do you realize we never cooked that bacon and eggs you promised me? I don't know why, but I'm almost madly hungry. And I ought not to stay much later; I don't want to compromise you on your very first night in the community. Towns like this—well, there's a gossipy old lady on every hilltop."

I scrambled out of bed. "Yes, and a doctor has to be like Caesar's Wife where women are concerned—that is, well above suspicion. Come down and I'll fix you some supper and then you must go." I felt strangely sorry for him. I had thrown myself in his arms, and unless he'd wanted to run like a rabbit there was nothing else he could have done. But what on earth had happened?

He scrambled into his clothes; I slipped into my denim robe, still wondering at myself. I'd known Roderick over a year before I'd agreed to go to bed with him.

"Bring the lamp along. I don't want to break my neck on those stairs in the dark," I said, "even though there's a doctor in the house."

The bedroom door closed behind us, cutting off the last vestige of the dizzying scent. Brian drew a deep breath and turned to me.

"Sara," he said, urgently, "I don't know what got into me. I never—listen, love. Before—before I came upstairs the second time, I was thinking that I wanted you, but I was going to take everything slow and easy, because this could be—be something very special. And now—" he shook his head in bewilderment.

I blinked, and said, "It was just as much of a surprise to me. I'm not—honestly, I'm *not* the kind of girl who falls into bed with men I've just met!" But even so, I was glad I had; I didn't think they made this kind of men any more.

"Are you—regretting it, Sara?"

"No," I said, honestly. "How could I regret anything like that?"

He leaned over and kissed me. "I'm not regretting it, either. It was one of the most marvelous—but good God, your Aunt Sara's perfume must really have a kick to it!"

He had spoken flippantly, but it struck instant awareness. "That *was* what started it, you know," I said. "Are there any herbs which are—aphrodisiac?"

He hesitated. "Not in the *standard* materia medica," he said. "Some doctors swear there isn't any such thing. I'm not so sure. Oh, hell, darling, let's not hunt for excuses. It happened and I'm not sorry. Let's get that bacon and eggs."

We laughed and teased each other while we moved around the big range, boiling water for tea, frying eggs and bacon in an enormous old iron frying pan; it was blackened and burnt, but the food tasted ambrosial. Nevertheless there was a little note of shrillness in our laughter; we were both surprised at ourselves, both uneasy. I hoped, unable to put it into words, that my sudden wanton behavior hadn't disillusioned him; he had enjoyed making love to me, he was being nice now—as any decent man would be—but would he decide that this was a one-time affair? I had enjoyed it unbelievably—but it would be too bad if he turned out a one-night stand instead of the friend I felt so much in need of.

We lingered over bacon and eggs and a second cup of tea, although he told me he rarely drank it. "I'm a coffee man, wench! What's the matter, don't you know that medical students *live* on coffee? I'll have to train you better," he said, and I felt hopeful again. But at last, when the clock in the hallway struck three—I found myself wondering who had wound it—he glanced regretfully at the door.

"Sara, I really must go. The rain has stopped and we really can't afford gossip at this stage. I hate to leave you alone, but—you *will* be all right?"

"Of course, Brian. You mustn't stay."

He kissed me, long and hard, and then I heard his car outside starting. After a long time I lifted the lamp and went slowly upstairs in the dark, where I crawled again into Aunt Sara's huge, lonely bed.

I half expected to lie awake, but I didn't. Once, in the dim light of early dawn, I half woke to hear a strange gnawing noise. Rats? Squirrels? Aunt Sara's ghost? I said aloud, "Oh, *blast* Aunt Sara," and fell asleep again.

FOUR

GINGER TOM

I WOKE TO SEE SUNLIGHT, WET AND WATERY, FILLING THE ROOM. For a moment, as I looked up in bewilderment at the thick white canopy overhanging the bed, I was confused about where I was; then memory rushed back and I remembered everything.

I went to the window, drawing back the heavy curtains. By daylight the ancient dark furniture looked even more heavy and forbidding, but the bed had been comfortable enough and I had slept well.

The Reverend Hay to the contrary, the house was not particularly dilapidated, even by—what was it—city standards. I don't know what he thought they were, but except for layers of dust, it seemed awfully well kept up. Had the—whatever—oh yes, "historical society" been keeping it up all these years, or was it simply well-built and weathertight?

Below me lay a tumbled stretch of neglected lawn filled with the stray heads of peeping dandelions. Beyond that, a low hedge, then a hilly field covered with low, grassy mounds and weathered grey stones. They touched a curious horror-filled half-memory; then I realized that the house overlooked a graveyard, so old that half the stones were collapsed and worn away. I found myself laughing, almost in hysteria. Why not? *Every* respectable haunted house looks down on a graveyard, it's in their union rules.

Was this old graveyard, then, the original Witch Hill?

Anyway, I wasn't superstitious and certainly everybody buried in that graveyard had been dead so long that even their dust was dust . . . at least they'd hardly be noisy neighbors!

Then I found myself wondering if Aunt Sara was buried there, slammed the curtain down, and went down to fix myself some breakfast.

The big old kitchen seemed far less forbidding by morning light; even Aunt Sara's portrait on the stairs seemed to smile at me. Exploring the pantry behind the kitchen, I discovered that the stone floor and dark shelves were several degrees cooler than everywhere else in the house, a primitive milk-cooling arrangement from the days before iceboxes and refrigerators. Hot tea, bread toasted over the gas fire and spread thickly with butter, and an egg in the old spider, made me feel far more like myself—I decided I would worry about cholesterol some other time. And a bath in the huge old iron tub, into which the water ran surprisingly hot ten minutes after I lit the ancient gas geyser, restored me to some semblance of the Sara I had been three weeks ago. I went down to wash up the dishes left over from breakfast—I really would have to arrange for another tank of gas some time very soon—thinking that afterward I would explore the house and find the best room for setting up my easel and paints—after all, I was here to work.

The room seemed damp, and I flung the back door open to let the sunlight stream in over the sill. I had expected to have to wrestle with hinges and bolts, but to my surprise the door swung open as if it had opened every day for the last seven years. Maybe the Historical Society had been in here—in which case I'd certainly have to change the lock. Or maybe it was just that the place was after all incredibly well built—and incredibly clean—except for the dust.

While I was drying the last dish I heard a loud, insistent meowing, and a large ginger cat walked into the kitchen, quite as if he belonged there.

He stopped at the foot of the pantry food safe, looking up at it with calm expectancy.

"Meow!" he demanded, and I laughed out loud.

"Okay, Tom Cat. What witch ever existed without her cat—only I thought a witch's cat ought to be black?" I poured him a saucer of milk, added a raw egg and a strip of leftover bacon. Placidly, accepting them as his due, he began lapping up his breakfast, then followed me from room to room, pausing now and again to jump on a piece of furniture and sniff at it, and when I went to make my bed, he wormed himself up against the pillow, purring loudly.

"Good grief, Tom Cat," I said, "you certainly are making yourself at home! What's the matter—did the cat grapevine tell you the haunted house was open for business again and there was an opening for a witch's cat? Did you think you could pass yourself off as a real genuine witch's cat because maybe I didn't know any better?"

He purred loudly, as if in answer.

"You're going to be a lot of company. Okay, Cat, you can stay until somebody with a better right claims you. If I have to live in a place like this—what am I going to call you?" I considered aloud, then remembered the gentle, mild-mannered vampire on the TV soap opera *Dark Shadows*. Barnabas Collins, the *gentlemanly* vampire.

"Come on, Barnabas," I ordered, "let's find a spot for the easel."

Quite as if he understood me, he bounded down from the bed, sauntered into the hall and stopped outside one of the empty rooms.

"In there? All right," I humored him, and followed him inside. It was a large, light room, empty except for a few old trunks, with an enormous north-facing window which would make it an excellent place to paint. I set up the easel, having to let Barnabas find out by experience that it would not support his weight (fortunately, when it tipped with him, he jumped clear) and fetched a pail, mop, and dust rags from downstairs to clean up the dust in the room. When I had the place clean and shining, I went downstairs for lunch—tomato sandwiches—and more milk for Barnabas. I sat down on the sunny doorstep to make out a shopping list, deciding to walk to Madison Corners this afternoon for supplies, turpentine, and plenty of cat food or fish—this near the ocean that should be no problem, there were probably plenty of fishermen who had trash fish they couldn't sell, which they'd give me for almost nothing.

I was jotting down a secondary list of things to be seen to on my first visit to Arkham—art supplies could certainly be had at the college bookstore at Miskatonic, see about antique dealers since I certainly didn't want all this surplus furniture, etc.—when a strange voice said almost over my head:

"Well, there, Ginger Tom! I see you've moved right in and made yourself at home!"

The cat meowed intelligently; I scrambled to my feet to greet the man who was coming around the side of the house.

He was very tall—probably a good six and a half feet—wearing somber, dark clothes. His face was razor-thin, his hair pale and untidy, and he had a long beaked nose and chin, and thick eyebrows below which his eyes gleamed steely blue. No, that isn't entirely right. All that makes him sound like a gargoyle, and he wasn't. He was human, and almost handsome; but in a rugged, steel-strong, old New England way. He looked like the figurehead of an old windjammer, or like the effigy of a Crusader knight on a tomb. I was to come to know him well; yet my artist's eye always saw him like that, as I had seen him the first time. Or was it really the first time? I slammed that thought out of my mind and tried to lock the door after it.

He stopped short, a few feet from me, and raised his eyes from the cat. His face paled.

"I heard in the village that you had come back," he said almost inaudibly. "Old Jeb told me. But he is a superstitious old fool—I never believed—"

I interrupted him sharply. "What on earth are you talking about? I've never been in this part of the world before in all my life, and this is the second time I've heard this nonsense about coming back! I see you know the cat; is he yours by any chance? He's a beautiful animal; I've been halfway expecting someone to turn up and claim him all morning."

The man gave his head a little shake. He looked confused, but was trying hard to conceal it. Finally he said, "No, no, Ginger Tom isn't my cat, but it's true I know him well; he was Miss Latimer's cat, and of course he and I are old friends."

I scowled disbelievingly. Barnabas was a fine young tomcat, but he could hardly be more than a year or so old; two at the very most. Aunt Sara had been dead seven years. I said, "If my Aunt Sara—Miss Latimer—owned a yellow tomcat like this one, it's quite likely he peopled the neighborhood with all kinds of ginger-colored kittens in his image. It's a nice coincidence, though, that a duplicate of Aunt Sara's cat should be waiting for me on the doorstep the very morning I move in. Forgive me, I'm chattering," I held out my hand. "My name is Sara Latimer."

He smiled faintly. "Yes, I know; your face is all the identification you need in these parts, Miss Latimer."

"Are there other Latimers in this neighborhood then?"

"Oh, no; I think you—or, I mean Miss Sara Latimer was the last—or at least I thought—or maybe I feared so. I am Matthew Hay, and you must forgive me; I knew your aunt—" he hesitated, "rather well for many years. Have you by any chance come to take her place?"

Now the name connected in my mind. *But her place at what?* I wondered. *His crazy church, whatever that was?*

"Mr. Hay," I said "you wrote my father about buying the house, but the letter reached me only after his death." His grip on my hand was strong, but the fingers felt ice-cold. "I thought I should come here to see the house before I decided to sell it. After all, if it's been in the family three hundred years, I hardly like to let it pass into strange hands."

Matthew Hay said, "I can understand that; your Aunt Sara felt much the same way. I had understood, however, that she had only distant relatives, and that none of them were interested in the property. I urged her many times to arrange that the house should be sold for a fair price to the Church after her death, but like most of us, Miss Sara had no true awareness of her own mortality, and she kept postponing it. After her death, I waited for several years in the hope that the house might again be occupied by—shall we say—a sympathetic member of her family. When no such event took place, I made inquiries about the legal owners of the property and made my offer. Yet now that you are here, and you are evidently one of the Latimers, perhaps—perhaps it will not be necessary."

I followed very little of this. It sounded as if he was rambling. Later, when I knew him better, I discovered that Matthew Hay never rambled, that every word he said went directly to his objective; but he was superb at concealing his objective from others.

I said, "The Church of the Antique Rite, Mr. Hay—is this a Catholic church?"

"Catholic only in the older sense of *universal*," he said. "Our church is far, far older than Christianity."

I translated, mentally: *nut-cult*. "Well," I said, "I'm not sure that I want to part with the house at all. It's been in the family far too long. In any case, I shan't even be thinking about selling this summer. I can't move again until my book is finished."

A strange look passed over his face. I thought for a moment that it was rage; but when he spoke again he sounded as bland as ever.

"Your Aunt Sara was a firm and dedicated member of our church—in fact, she was a real leader," he said. "There have been

Latimers active in our work since they first came to this country in the sixteen-hundreds. The first Sara Latimer was a martyr to ignorant persecution of our religion."

The first Sara Latimer was hanged as a witch.

"Are you trying to tell me that your church is—is a witch-cult? That you worship the Devil?"

"Miss Latimer, only the ignorant call it by that name. At your present level of knowledge I cannot even discuss it with you," he said. "Perhaps when you know more about our religion—and it is a true religion—you may wish to affiliate with us. As I told you, Miss Sara, your great-aunt, was one of our greatest leaders. She was greatly respected, one might even say revered, in our community. But today I came only to welcome you to Madison Corners, and to ask if there is anything I can do to make you more comfortable here."

With a twinkle of mischief, I thought, *Thank you, but Brian Standish has already welcomed me to the house.* "You're very kind; I would like to know where I can buy eggs and milk, and where I can order more bottled gas for cooking."

"Miss Latimer always bought her milk at the Whitfield farm, which you pass on your way to the bus stop," Matthew Hay told me, "and if you're not interested in gardening, they can probably supply you with green vegetables and garden stuff, too. She had an excellent herb garden, which I fear has fallen into neglect, although I confess, Miss Latimer, that I have come here from time to time to collect herbs, and have tried to do what little I can, to keep it up. The old New England herb lore is rapidly being lost to humanity, and I think it is well worth preserving. Also—" he smiled, and his bleak face looked suddenly human and kindly, "I confess that I suffer from time to time with rheumatism and colds, and I find her herbal remedies better than the pills and potions our local doctor dishes out. I hope you will forgive my trespass."

"Please come whenever you like," I said swiftly. "I didn't even know Aunt Sara had an herb garden; I've had no time to explore the garden, I don't even know how much land goes with the house."

"Then please let me volunteer my services to show you around the property," Matthew Hay said. "I have known this property since my childhood; in fact, I am your neighbor." He gestured past the old graveyard. "My house is beyond that grove of trees. You can't see it from here. Let me show you the gardens."

I accompanied him around the corner of the house; the cat Barnabas, who had curled up on the stone step sunning himself, uncoiled his yellow legs and stalked ceremoniously after us. I caught Matthew Hay looking back surreptitiously at the cat. There was something catlike in him, too; his almost animal grace, the feline strength of his shoulders. His hands were enormous, even for his six-foot-plus height.

"Here is the garden; the herbs are here in the sun along the fence," Matthew Hay said. The fence was grey and weathered, although in excellent repair. I sniffed the air, which was fragrant in the hot sun as the slender, straight rows and little round patches of herbs gave off their scent.

"I recognize thyme and savory," I said, "and lavender and verbena." I stooped and picked one of the small sprigs of lemon-scented leaves, crushing them between my fingers. "But none of the others."

"Here is comfrey," he said. "It was called Knitbone, because many people believe that, used in poultices and tea, it hastens the healing of a fracture. Many people believed that your late great-aunt knew more about such things than doctors. For instance she suggested to me that rosemary—" he leaned over to pluck a few leaves, "was an excellent cure for baldness. I have used it as a hair lotion for years, and as you can see, I still have all my hair, even though my father went bald at forty."

I smiled, "I'll have to keep up the herb garden." *Maybe Brian would be interested, too; many doctors, I knew, made some use of herbs, and old-fashioned remedies.*

"That decision, at least, I applaud. I'll be happy to help you, and teach you what I know," he said.

A curious, intoxicating scent was stealing up from a small patch of green leaves; a scent I recognized as at least one component of the strange perfume in the porcelain jar that had affected Brian and me so strangely last night. I picked a few of the small, spiky leaves, and held it out in my hand to Matthew Hay. "What is this?" I demanded sharply. "I slept last night in Aunt Sara's room—and this scent was all over it."

"Tarragon," he said. "Made into tea, it is said to be good for digestive upsets and flatulence."

I frowned faintly. "My mother used to put tarragon in salads, and in vinegar," I said, "and it doesn't smell anything like that."

He crushed a few of the leaves between his fingers. The scent was strangely disturbing and unsettling. He said, slowly, his eyes resting narrowly on me, "The smell of fresh herbs is not at all like the dried ones you buy in supermarkets. They are often diluted with cheaper weeds."

I crushed the leaves between my fingers, as he had done, and smelled them. Breathing the scent deeply, I discovered that it had a strange effect on me. My clothes seemed confining and tight, as if my skin craved fresh air. Every nerve of my body seemed more alive. Looking up, I found Matthew Hay's eyes resting on me, still with that disturbing, avid glance.

I wonder what he's like in bed! He looks strong, powerful . . .

Matthew Hay said, with quiet emphasis, "It is also believed to be an aphrodisiac—a sexual stimulant."

I dropped the leaves as if they had burned me, but he was laughing.

My eyes fastened on a low bush at the end of the garden, laden with heavy, blue-black berries. "Are those blueberries?" I asked.

"Hardly!" He drew me back as I was about to touch them. "I wouldn't advise you to use them in a pie, Miss Latimer! Those are belladonna—deadly nightshade! The active element is atropine!"

I drew back. "What are they doing in an herb garden?"

"Carefully used, in small quantities," he said, "they can be used as a—a psychedelic. They have also some small medical use. Otherwise, they are deadly poison."

He moved on, pointing out to me the other herbs. Thyme, lemon thyme and savory, used in cooking; mugwort, a cure for acne and warts; marjoram, to relieve dropsy and swelling, as well as a superb seasoning for fish or chicken; fennel, for relieving the summer diarrheas which used to carry off so many small children in the community; and other herbs whose names were strange to me. Their scents, bitter, intoxicating or sweetly pungent, blended after a time into a whirl in my mind and senses. I was interested to find a patch of catnip around. If Aunt Sara had had a similar cat, and if she had grown the catnip for his benefit, he—well, he certainly walked in it as if he owned it.

As we came to the end of the garden, Matthew Hay said, "Would you care to see my church? It is just past the graveyard—in fact, this graveyard was once the 'buryin' ground,' as the old New Englanders called it, back when this was the official Puritan church; in those days it was called the Separatist Church of Christ, the same group which is now known as the Congregational church all over New England. I usually cut through the graveyard, coming here; I trust you have no superstitious fears? Many women would not care to live alone in a house overlooking a graveyard." He ushered me through the ruined gate.

"My father used to say: why be afraid of the dead, when there are so many living people more able to harm us?"

"A sensible man, as far as he went," said Matthew Hay, deftly evading an old, half-fallen grave I had not seen before.

It occurred to me that some of my ancestors must be buried here. "Are there any Latimers in this graveyard?"

"A great many. Miss Latimer—your great-aunt—expressed a

wish to be buried here beside her forefathers, but this graveyard is no longer open for burials, and she is buried—officially—in the grave-yard at Madison Corners Church."

"What do you mean—officially?" I demanded, and the curious look of rage flitted over his face again. He clenched his hands until the knuckles popped white. I thought, for a moment, that he was going to hit me, and I actually flinched. But he quickly mastered his voice.

"I mean that Miss Latimer often said that she loved this place so that she was sure her spirit would return here, no matter where her body lay," he said. "Here is one of your ancestresses, Sara."

I looked down, and a cold chill of horror ran through me:

SARA MAGDALEN LATIMER
Savaged here by dogs, 1884
"And the dogs did eat her flesh" II Kings ix, 36

"Oh, God!" I burst out, "I dreamed about that last night! I saw that . . ."

Matthew Hay's hands were hard and firm, supporting me. "It's a well-known text."

"But we never were a Bible-reading family," I gasped, "and it's not the sort of thing I'd think of . . ."

"Don't be worried," he said soothingly, "you may not have dreamed it at all. There is a phenomenon called *déjà vu,* where you believe you've seen something before; most psychologists now be-lieve it simply means that one half of your brain perceives it before the other half, so that it seems familiar. Or possibly, as you came into the house last night, you perceived it at the bare edge of your visual field, and your subconscious remembered it, even though you didn't."

I shook my head, stubbornly. Last night when I arrived at the house it had been so dark that I'd needed the flashlight even to get in-side. "No. I dreamed it. This damn house!"

"I think you're overwrought," he said. "Do you want to go back?

I warned you that living so near a graveyard might damage your nerves."

Now he'll be after me again to sell the house. "No," I said. I turned around and looked at the house in full daylight. Now it was only a ridiculously ugly old building, which had evidently begun with an old New England salt-box, and future generations had built on long, rambling wings, turrets, balconies, bay windows, without rhyme or reason or architectural good sense. It was a monstrosity which would make an artist run away screaming, and now, by daylight, it only looked laughable. In Berkeley it would have been thought of as a masterpiece of high camp. Witches, old religions, haunted houses, cats on the doorstep—it was all a high-camp nightmare, and I laughed.

"A house like that would give anybody nightmares," I said. "Let's see the rest of the graveyard. Are there any funny old epitaphs?"

"Quite a few, as it happens," Matthew Hay said. "This place would be a tourist trap if it became known. For instance, here is one of my own ancestresses." He led me to an ancient, grey marble gravestone, and helped me decipher the crumbling letters:

GOODWIFE TABITHA HAY

Died 1702

Beloved Wife of The-Lord-Is-My-Repose Hay
The Lord Giveth and the Lord Taketh Away
Blessed Be the Lord.

"I don't see anything very funny about that," I said, "although— what a name! The-Lord-Is-My-Repose!"

"Some of them had worse names than that," Matthew Hay said. "The old family Bible lists one of my great-great-grandfathers as Fight-the-Good-Fight-for-the-Lord Hay. But you haven't seen it all yet. The old fellow had three wives. Look, here's wife number two."

This tombstone read:

ELIZA HAY

Died 1709

Wife of The-Lord-Is-My-Repose Hay
It Is Better to Marry than to Burn.

"He evidently didn't burn," I commented. "Where's wife number three?"

"Over here."

CHARITY HAY

Died 1714

Wife of The-Lord-Is-My-Repose Hay
If a woman would be virtuous, let her be a virgin.

"Good heavens!" I gasped. "What an epitaph on a man's wife!"

"But here's the climax," said Matthew Hay, leading me to a tall, grey monument, pointing with phallic power at the sky, "here's the old man himself."

THE-LORD-IS-MY-REPOSE HAY

Died April 1, 1754

It is better to dwell in a corner of the housetop
than in a wide house with a brawling woman.

I couldn't help laughing. "The old rascal!"

"Oh, well, he may have had good reason for becoming a misogynist," Matthew Hay commented.

Shared laughter had taken away a good deal of my unease; I now felt quite at home with this man and by the time we had explored the graveyard, commenting pityingly on the many children who died before they were two, on the quaint old names and Bible texts, we were calling one another "Matthew" and "Sara."

I was no longer startled when I found two or three other tombstones where a "Sara Latimer" lay buried, from 1657 up to 1908. There were other Hays, Standishes, Latimers, Whitfields, Whateleys, Marshes, and a multitude of names famous in the history of New England. At the far end of the graveyard, where there was a weathered old bronze archway, he led me out across the small grove of trees toward an ancient, crumbling old stone building.

"The Church of the Antique Rite."

"Surely the building is old enough to be dangerous." I hesitated on the steps before going in.

"The craftsmen of those days built more carefully than modern ones," he said, "and a church, especially, was built for all time. In Europe, many cathedrals built in the tenth century are still in daily use. The longer a church stands, the more powerful it is—the accumulated worship of all the past collects and creates an aura of power."

His hand on my arm urged me inside. I thought: witch-cult? No, it can't be, if it's held in a genuine consecrated church. I went inside.

The church was old, and a musty smell of ancient wood and stone overwhelmed me, combined with a curious odor of herbs and something else I did not recognize. There were no pews, or else they had all been taken away. After a step or two, I felt strangely queasy, unwilling to go further. His grip on my arm was strangely compelling; he led me straight up to the altar.

It was low and flat, a slab like one of the tombstones; several things lay on it; a cup, a green willow wand.

I felt as if a mist was passing before my eyes. I asked, sharply, "Where is the black handled knife?"

His voice rasped; "I thought you told me you knew nothing of these things!" He whirled on me, his eyes gleaming like blazing steel.

I shook my head, feeling dazed. "I don't. I swear I don't. I haven't any idea how I came to say such a thing!"

"But I do!" He whirled to face me, his hands gripping my shoulders. His breath was hot in my face. "Sara Latimer, you are one of us! Your innermost memory tells you that you are one of us! Can't you see? Every time a girl with your physical and emotional characteristics has been born into your family, she has been a great priestess of the Old Religion! And now that you have come here, the ancestral memory is strong in you, too!" His voice dropped to a compelling murmur. "Haven't you found that since you came here, you have been saying and doing strange things, things which you would never have done before?"

That made me stop and think. I had found myself in bed, last night, with a total stranger. I struggled weakly, saying, "I don't want to be a witch!"

"You say that because you know nothing of it," Matthew said, and held me firmly. "It is your destiny now, Sara. You are one of us. You cannot fight it."

"No! No!" I tried to wrench free. But his warm breath was dizzying, the touch of his hands, hard and cruel as it was, strangely exciting.

He said, in a low, compelling tone, "Let us consecrate the homecoming of our priestess."

I could not draw away. As if hypnotized, I let him draw off my skirt and blouse. He threw aside his own clothes and stood before me, raising his arms in a strange ritual gesture.

"Dark Goat of the Woods! Horned One of Lust and Power! Witness that I take this woman, thy neophyte, in homage to thee!"

I heard myself whispering, dazed:

"So mote it be!"

His body was tall, narrowly built and almost hairless, but the muscles in back and chest rippled smoothly, like a cat's, as he strode toward me. He was fully erect and looked enormous, the male organ long and hard, seeming to pulse to some curious rhythm. *This is in-*

sane, I thought, *the man's mad!* No, I am mad. *We're all mad here! And there's the Cheshire cat!* Over Matthew's shoulder I saw Barnabas, who had hopped up on the altar and lay there surveying us with wide, wicked yellow eyes.

I heard myself moan aloud as a wave of desire swept over me, something I could not control. Matthew's hands closed over my breasts, crushing painfully down, and I felt the tips harden and swell. He pushed me back and down until I lay on the stone floor at the foot of the altar, and knelt there astride me, crying out words I did not understand;

"Ad baraldim, asdo galoth Azathoth!"

I wanted to scream, to cry out, to claw at him and scramble to my feet and run away, run away naked if it must be, run away through the graveyard naked, run and run and run and never stop—

He bent down, and bit me savagely on the breast. I heard myself cry out, a low frenzied cry. His mouth moved along my body, nibbling, biting, sucking fiercely; lingered on the belly, moved inexorably downward. He raised himself again, and gasped, his voice breaking:

"I do homage to the gateway of life!"

Slowly, deliberately, as if performing some curious ritual, his mouth came down toward the soft opened parts of my spread legs. It closed, lingered there, half bite, half lingering kiss; I moaned aloud, frenzied, only half aware of what was happening.

Then he flung himself upright, his face distorted, his eyes glowing as green as the cat's, and lowered himself over me. Roughly his hard hands parted my thighs and I felt him ram into me, hard, painfully, striking deep into the roots of my body. I cried out and began to struggle, but his hands gripped me so hard I could not move. Again and again, savagely, he struck hard and deep, again and again and again, until the pain merged into response, and I felt myself moving, writhing, clawing, hardly knowing now whether I was fighting fiercely to escape or joining him in wild response. Then I

knew, and I heard myself scream, madly, mindlessly, my body whip-
ping back and forth, my hands clawing, leaving blood on his naked
back and shoulders, my legs gripping over his back. We swayed back
and forth together, rocking, gasping, his face contorted and mad, and
a red-streaked haze swayed and folded down before my eyes. The cat
let out a long, wild, echoing wail, and jumped down from the altar
and thrust his nose against our joined heads.

I lay back, struggling for breath, my heart pounding, while
Matthew rose slowly to his knees. He went to the altar, stretching out
his hands above it, muttering to himself or to whatever strange Gods
he was invoking.

Shaken, half crying, I groped for my clothes. Barnabas poked his
nose against my hand, and I patted him absent-mindedly. *Damn it,* I
thought, *I must be going out of my mind.*

What could I do? Make outraged noises of protest? Unless
Matthew Hay were completely out of his senses, he surely knew I'd
enjoyed it as much as he had. But what in the world—or the devil—
had gotten into me?

Matthew came back, bending down to touch my hair lightly. He
said gently. "Welcome to us, Beloved."

I realized that I was still under the curious spell, whatever it was.
A strange picture came into my mind, and I said, not clearly aware of
just why, "This was wrong, Matthew. You were not wearing the mask
of the Horned One."

His eyes gleamed in jubilation. He said, "Now you know that
you are really one of us. The Mask does not matter, Sara; we shall
make up for it at the Esbat tomorrow night, now that you have been
sealed to me. We can introduce you to the coven then, and you can
take your old place as our priestess."

Barnabas's head was still under my hand; it felt warm, an island
of sanity and normalcy in a mad mirage-laden universe. The world
still spun under me, and I felt weak and dizzy, my body warm and
sated. But somehow I must come back to reality. I got my legs under

me and half rose, pulling my wrap-around skirt around my waist and buckling it. I drew my sweater over my head, welcoming the momentary darkness as it covered my eyes. When my head emerged, I tossed back my damp hair and looked steadily at Matthew.

"I don't know how you did that," I said, "but it doesn't mean what you think it means."

"No?" He sat down, cross-legged, still naked before his great altar. Most men look ridiculous afterward, with their sex limp and dangling, but Matthew still held a curious residue of power and strength. He said, "Answer me truthfully, Sara. Have you ever done anything like this before—ever in your life?"

I knew perfectly well what he meant. But I didn't answer the question he was asking. "Have I had sex, do you mean? Of course; I'm twenty-three years old and it's 1971. No girl is a virgin at my age unless she's so full of hangups she's impossible. I lived with a man in California for almost a year."

His eyes were steady, not regarding the evasion. "That wasn't what I asked. I mean, like this; easily, promiscuously, without any of the romantic pretensions of our culture."

It was the very thing I had been thinking about. A girl might go to bed—once—with a total stranger, a man she had met only an hour or so before, and it might mean, only, a sudden overpowering attraction. I had been wondering, this very morning, if with Brian it had been love at first sight. But to do this twice, to jump into bed—or at least into sex—with a perfect stranger twice in twenty-four hours, this was something else. It wasn't me, it wasn't the kind of thing I did.

Just the same, I wasn't going to tell him about Brian. He might call himself a priest but that didn't mean he had any right to hear my confession. I said evasively, "Not before I came here, no. Never."

His eyes were still level and steady. It was certainly the strangest post-sex conversation I'd ever had with a man. He asked, "And do you feel guilty?"

Guilty? "No," I said honestly, "not really. But I do feel—well, foolish. A little ashamed. It seems a stupid and tasteless thing to do."

"Why?"

I had no answer ready; and although I still didn't know what to make of this strange madman who seemed able to read my mind and my very soul, I wasn't going to stoop to lie to him. I said, "I don't know. I'll have to think about it. I'll have to decide what I really feel." I rose to my feet. I felt a little better looking down on him. He scrambled up, too, and leisurely reached for his clothes.

He said, "What you're feeling now is simply readjustment from your old self—your false upbringing—to the real you, the witch-self, Sara. All witches are promiscuous, and take their pleasure where they please."

"What makes you think this is my real self?"

He smiled. "Look at the painting in your house, Sara. Every Sara Latimer is a witch."

He put his hand under my elbow to guide me out of the church. When I moved I felt a reminiscent stir inside my body; but I shut out awareness of it. I said, with a sudden flare of anger, "You didn't use anything; what do I do if you've made me pregnant? Or isn't a witch supposed to care about a little thing like that?"

He threw back his head and laughed, doing up his trousers. At my stare of angry outrage, he stopped laughing and said kindly, "I'm sorry, Sara; I keep forgetting how little your conscious self knows of these things. One of the great truths of witchcraft is that—unless it is done deliberately as a fertility ritual, which this wasn't—no witch ever left the Black Altar, as the saying goes, carrying anything she didn't bring with her."

I hoped that was a fact, and not just a belief of the witch-cult! He must have sensed my skepticism, for he said, "I suppose you'll have to wait and see, then, unless your full witch-memory returns. I'm sorry you have to worry about it; believe me, it's not necessary." He finished knotting his necktie. He looked cool, civilized, and neat, with no sign of the savage frenzy of a bare five minutes ago.

He escorted me back across the graveyard, and to the door of the old house. "I have preparations to make," he said, "and I must speak with others of the coven. Forgive me if I leave you now. But I will see you again at the Esbat."

I let him go without a word and watched him as he went away, smiling and jaunty. But the—childish and nasty—valedictory phrase of schoolgirls was ringing in my mind. "See me at the Esbat? *Not if I see you first!*"

FIVE

MY OWN TRUE LOVE

INSIDE THE HOUSE I WENT UPSTAIRS, AVOIDING THE PAINTED EYES of Aunt Sara on the staircase. *Every witch is promiscuous.* Had she lured the local men to her bed, even when she was an old hag? Oh, hell, who was I to criticize? I wasn't going to give myself any easy rationalizations, or say I'd been hypnotized, or any of that nonsense. Okay, so I screwed Matthew Hay—I put it as crudely as I could. I'd enjoyed it. But if I started believing I was possessed by the soul, or souls, of some witch or other in my family, that way lay a fast ride to the local funny-farm!

Upstairs, I climbed into the high tin tub and scrubbed and scrubbed, angrily trying to wash away the scent, and the memory, of Matthew Hay's body. My breasts were bruised and darkening fast; there were teethmarks on my shoulder, and blood under my fingernails where I'd clawed him. When I finally got out and toweled myself dry, I went into my bedroom and dug into my suitcase for first-aid cream, carefully avoiding all the little porcelain pots and jars on Aunt Sara's dresser. I'd better get rid of them, no matter how good her herbal remedies were. I remembered reading that there was no such thing as a real aphrodisiac—but *something* had certainly touched off Brian last night. And me, too.

I went into the room I'd chosen as a studio, got out a piece of drawing paper and pinned it on the easel, and tried to begin one of the illustrations. It wasn't any good; I found myself idly sketching a curious, horned mask . . . the mask of the Horned One? Whatever *that* was!

Lonely and dejected, I found myself half inclined to pack my suitcase again and flee down the road. The Arkham bus would be going by in about half an hour. This house was just too much for me. Barnabas mewed downstairs, and I went down and fed him the last of the milk. Another complication; now that the beast had adopted me, I couldn't simply leave him to starve. Oh, damn it, if I was really a witch, I ought to be able to summon someone to take care of the cat, or cast a spell that would bring someone to come and cheer me up!

I wandered disconsolately around the house. In the big book-lined library, I found a volume that looked about a hundred years old, entitled *The God of the Witches*: leafing through it, I happened on the information that the Esbat was the weekly meeting of a witch-coven, and a Sabbat their four-times-yearly festival. That reminded me of Matthew Hay again, and I thrust the book back on its shelf. Maybe I ought to read it and find out just what I was up against, but not now.

Suddenly my mood brightened; I've never been psychic, but I found myself whistling cheerfully, and I wasn't really surprised when a familiar little dark-blue Volkswagen chugged up the hill and stopped in the driveway.

It was like a weight rolling off my heart. I hadn't realized how much I'd feared that he'd think of me just as an "easy lay" and not a girl he really liked, who wanted to know him better. I ran to the front door and opened it as he came up on the porch.

"Oh, Brian, I'm *glad* to see you!"

He put out his arms and hugged me. "Hullo, green-eyed witch! You look beautiful! I'd have dropped around before, but I had to stop

and check over a girl with measles, and an old man who got his finger caught in a mousetrap, as well as a few others of the ills flesh is
heir to. But I kept remembering you, and trying to think of a good
excuse to come up here and see you, and I finally found one."

"I can't imagine why you thought you needed one," I said. He
blushed. "Well, I didn't want you to think I was just trying to—well,
to talk you into bed again. But as it happens, I did think of a perfectly good excuse. Do you realize that I lighted the lamp for you and
never taught you how to light it for yourself? I was afraid it would
get dark and you would still be struggling with the wick and the
burner!"

"That's a *marvelous* excuse!" *And as for talking me into bed again,
what makes you think you need to?* But I didn't say that. I felt somewhat
abashed, wondering suddenly if the sex with Brian had been real—
or, like what I'd had with Matthew Hay, simply a reflex of the witch-
influence? Oh, *rubbish!* I'd wanted Brian. I hadn't wanted Matthew
Hay, and I wasn't going to let him keep me away from Brian.

"Come in, Brian."

"You couldn't keep me out." He stepped inside and met the wide
eyes of Barnabas. "Hullo, have you found yourself a pet already,
Sara?"

"He seems to have found me, instead; he turned up on the doorstep as if he owned the house. Brian, when you leave, can you drive
me down to the store? I need cat food, and a few more groceries."

"I've got a better idea than that. I'll go shopping with you—I'm
more likely than you to know what you'll need in a house like this—
and then we'll drive somewhere down the coast and have dinner, a
regular shore dinner with crab and lobster and that sort of goodies,
and then—well, we'll see; unless the hospital in Arkham calls me up
with some sort of emergency, we'll think up some way to spend the
evening."

I ran upstairs to fetch my handbag. It was a relief to shut the
house door behind me, even to get out of sight of the wide, knowing

eyes of Barnabas. I had expected to end up at the general store in Madison Corners, but instead he drove along the road to Arkham, taking me into a big modern supermarket near the campus. While we guided the cart through the aisles, picking up foods that would not spoil without refrigeration, I learned that he had been born in Madison Corners, and graduated from Miskatonic here before going away to medical school in Boston after a brief hitch in the Army.

"Like almost any graduate doctor these days, I could set up in a big city—where the already have plenty of doctors—and get into heavy competition for the nice fat practice. Most of my classmates even in medical school thought I was some kind of nut, to settle for a country practice out here at the back of beyond; even Arkham is isolated enough, and all those farms back toward Innsmouth, they're right off the map!"

I remembered the bus driver's statement, "*Nobody* wants to go to Innsmouth."

"Is there something wrong with the place?"

He shrugged. "I suppose not. The local population is a mishmash of old New England stock—old enough to have degenerated through inbreeding, incest and God-knows-what-all—South Sea Islanders, Portuguese fishermen who've been here long enough to qualify as Old New England themselves, and all sorts and conditions of the dregs of the world's seaports. Innsmouth used to be a major seaport along this coast. The town is crumbling, the fishing business has gone elsewhere, and so has every inhabitant with enough intelligence and energy to pick up and go. What's left is practically the dregs of humanity. But they get sick too, and except for Cousin James, who's getting on toward seventy, and a senile old chap out at Whateley's Crossing, I'm the only doctor outside Arkham in this part of the state. I've never been able to see why it's virtuous to go and spend one's life bringing the troubles of civilization to the starving Biafrans or Pakistanis, and at the same time it's called plain stupid to spend a few years in Appalachia or out in the boondocks of New England."

He glared at me almost defensively. "And if you say I'm a fuzzy-minded idealist, I'll—I'll—"

"Kiss me, I hope," I said softly, and squeezed his arm. "I think it's wonderful, Brian."

"It's not *wonderful*," he said, gruffly defensive, "it's just *necessary*, and nobody else is doing it." He turned on me and grinned. "But I admit it was pretty grim until you turned up, and I'm going to appeal to your social conscience to spend a lot of time with me, and keep me happy so I'll feel like staying here."

"That will be a pleasure," I said, and meant it, "but I thought that in this nice healthy unspoiled farm country there'd be a nice, uninhibited country girl behind every haystack."

"But that's what I'm telling you," Brian said. "This isn't nice healthy unspoiled farm country, this is degeneracy and decadence, Sara. Some of these old, old families are so inbred that there are a couple of halfwits—lethal recessives, congenital defectives—born into almost every family. I suspect the local index of mental illness is higher than it is even under stresses of urban life such as in Harlem. Did you think it was just local superstition that called your Aunt Sara a witch, or says that the local folks are queer?"

I smiled crookedly. "I hope the house doesn't affect me that way."

"I didn't mean that. Your branch of the family must be relatively healthy; they escaped. But the ones who stayed here got queerer and queerer, and that goes for the Standishes and the Whitefields and the Marshes and the Hays just as much as for the Latimers. I wouldn't be surprised if some of the local folks were nutty enough to believe in witchcraft or hex stuff, and practice it, too."

This brought be straight back to Matthew Hay. *I will see you again at the Esbat*. I couldn't discuss that with Brian. He might think none the less of me for jumping into bed with *him* at first sight, he evidently shared the attraction, but how would he feel if I tried to tell him that Matthew Hay had also hypnotized me to the point where I'd lain with him on the floor in his screwball church?

We wheeled the shopping cart around the corner, to a pile of canned pumpkin, and bumped into another cart. The man behind it whirled, stared, then a familiar voice—a voice I associated with that other life three thousand miles away—said, "Why, it's Sally Latimer, isn't it?"

The man pushing the cart was tall and slightly built, with grey hair and a paradoxical look of extreme strength. I was not at all displeased to see a familiar face.

"Dr. MacLaran," I exclaimed.

"A friend, Sara?" Brian asked. "I didn't think you knew anyone in this part of the country."

"I don't. I can't imagine—excuse me; Colin MacLaran, Dr. Brian Standish."

"She called you Dr. MacLaran—" Brian began.

"Ph.D. only," Colin MacLaran said. "I keep forgetting; undergraduates in this country keep calling every college instructor Doctor, whether they are or not. Just one of the strange things about American undergraduates. I don't think they do it in Europe."

"But what are you doing in this part of the world?"

"I'm lecturing in folklore—at Miskatonic University—for the summer session," Colin said. "I ran into Roderick at the bookstore and he told me you'd gone back east to nurse your mother. How is she, Sally?"

"She died about two weeks ago," I said. Had it been only that long? I was shocked.

"Oh. I'm sorry," he said. That was the thing about Colin MacLaran; it wasn't a mere social noise, one got the impression that he really was sorry. "I hope the rest of your family is well.'

When I told him briefly about the deaths of Brad and my father he looked horrified.

"What a dreadful thing, Sally! You have other family living hereabouts, then? For me of course it's strictly business, but this seems a fairly bleak part of the world—"

"Family here from the year One, I guess," I said. "I've inherited the most god-awful old place out on Witch Hill Road—a regular haunted house—the place is crawling with local tradition—if you're really interested in local folklore you ought to come out and have a look at it, maybe collect the local stories about the place."

"I'd really like to," he said, "but just now I mustn't keep you young people—Witch Hill: that's out near Madison Corners, right?"

"That's right," I said. "And there's an old church out there—something called the Church of the Antique Rite—it ought to be right up your alley."

"I've heard about some of those old churches," he said thoughtfully. "I really should come out and have a look if you wouldn't mind."

"I'd love it," I said, with considerable relief; I might have no relatives left here—but wasn't it strange that one of my oldest friends should turn up here—of all places?

SIX

OLD FRIENDS

"I REALLY WOULD LOVE TO HAVE YOU COME," I SAID, "BUT RIGHT now Brian has to get back to the hospital—"

"Of course," Colin said, but Brian interrupted. "It'll only take me ten minutes or so; why don't you stay and talk to the professor while I check up. Then, if you'd like—" he hesitated. "Maybe you'd like to join us for dinner, sir."

"I'd like that very much," Colin said, "but only if you'll allow me to be your host." He laughed. "And Sally can tell me all about her haunted house."

He laughed again, to let me know he was being facetious; but it occurred to me that if anyone could make sense of my unbelievable legacy, it would be Colin MacLaran.

I asked him, "Who's taking care of the bookstore while you're out here? Claire?"

"Oh, no. Claire is here with me as a teaching assistant," he told us. "I left the store in Paul Frederick's hands—you remember Paul, don't you?"

"I think so; isn't he the tall skinny blond the kids call Frodo?"

"That's the one; he makes antique instruments, and it's not much of a living," Colin said. "And he's just gotten married, so he and Emily were happy to spend the summer baby-sitting the bookstore. Well, then, go ahead and check up at the hospital, and we'll join you there in the parking lot. I don't suppose there's more than one hospital in town?"

Brian laughed. "It's the only hospital in this end of the state," he said. "Anyone who has anything more serious than a dogbite has to go in by ambulance to Boston." He leaned over and kissed me lightly. "See you later, Sara—Sally," he amended.

I nodded. "Thanks; I really prefer it. Everyone on the Coast calls me that, and *Sara* is still the picture in the hallway up in that house."

He went off to his car and Colin said, "A nice young man, Sally."

"He is," I said fervently.

"If you'll forgive my saying so," Colin said, "he seems a little more your type than Roderick."

"I hope so," I said, and turned to pluck a dozen eggs out of the refrigerator case. I didn't really want to talk about that, even with Colin.

I bought cat food and another half-cart of groceries, and moved toward the checkstand; Colin was already there. His grocery cart looked sparsely filled, the sort of thing a single man might buy for solitary breakfasts and lunches. I realized I should be glad for having Brian to cook for sometimes.

Colin loaded my groceries into a Chevrolet Citation; I saw the rental sticker on it.

"Where are you staying, Colin?"

"Tourist cabin on the edge of Arkham; place almost qualifies as a historical landmark itself, but it's clean and there's a stove and refrigerator for what little cooking I do."

He put the car in gear, and drove toward the lighted parking lot that proclaimed ARKHAM GENERAL HOSPITAL.

I asked him, cautiously, "Do you know a man named Matthew Hay?"

"I hardly know the man but I'd bet that he's crazy as a crumpet," Colin said. "He's supposed to be pastor of some church or other I never heard of, probably hellfire-and-damnation or nut-cult; the reputable churches no longer bother to keep up congregations out here, although there is a Presbyterian church at Madison Corners. I don't imagine it will stay long; the minister looks pretty hungry. Why, have you met Hay?"

"He says he's a neighbor of mine; he passed by," I said. "He seems to know Barnabas, but I believe he thought for a time that he was Aunt Sara's own cat."

"I told you; crazy as a crumpet," Colin repeated. "Your Aunt Sara's been dead seven years, and I wonder if he thought the cat's been hanging around all that time? Or that the cat came back to life just for you?"

"I gather that for a while he actually believed I was my Aunt Sara," I said. "It's unnerving. In that house—I almost feel as if I *were* haunted by Aunt Sara! You *don't* suppose I am? I wonder if she was—was promiscuous?"

It was as near as I could come to putting my thoughts into words, but Colin laughed. "I wouldn't know; from the few times I saw the lady, I doubt very much if anyone would have cared whether she was or not. I know if she made a pass at *me* I'd probably have run a mile from the old witch. Oh, it wasn't *that* bad, she was remarkably well preserved, I understand, but not to the point where I'd have cared to investigate her sex life. Don't let the place get on your nerves." It occurred to me that Colin was remarkably well-informed for a newcomer to the area.

"Just the same, Sara, I'd steer clear of Matthew Hay. That fellow gives me the creeps. He has a sister or aunt or whatever, some old crone who keeps house for him—I think her name's Judith—and if your Aunt Sara had a reputation as a witch, that old dame—Judith Hay—is the three weird sisters from *Macbeth,* all wrapped up into one!"

"You don't think—"

"No, but I don't *know,* and if old Hay is a neighbor of Aunt Sara—the house could be fairly free of dust for a house that had been shut up for seven years. It just might be that Hay or the old lady has a key. If I were you I'd bolt the door at night on the inside, locks or no locks, just in case the old man gets to wandering."

"Thanks. I'll check the bolts."

"I wish, instead of the cat, that you had a good fierce well-trained dog."

So did I. I thought of Aunt Sara's room, smelling of her aphrodisiac perfume which seemed to rouse all my latent sexual desires. I thought of Matthew Hay, armed with a key given him by Aunt Sara—and now the problem of the relatively clean house was solved, and I would have the locks changed, next day, as soon as I could get around to it—there must be a locksmith in town. I found myself thinking of Matt Hay slipping up the stairs while I lay sleeping and paralyzed by the erotic perfume in the huge old four-poster. I thought of Matthew Hay naked, hairless, lithe and evil as—as Barnabas himself—or better yet, like a sleek panther in the zoo—gloating over my naked and senseless body, swooping down on me like a hawk on a chicken, with his huge and cruel sexuality, his glittering eyes, his harsh grasping hands . . .

But I couldn't tell Colin about that; I couldn't even tell Brian.

I came back to shocked awareness, realizing that I had not been able to put Matthew Hay out of my mind after all. I wasn't going to think of him again!

Brian came out of the hospital, saying swiftly, "Looks like I'm free for the evening—maybe for the night." He got into his car and I followed him with Colin. As we drove through the Arkham streets Colin pointed out to me many of the ancient houses, old gambrel- and mansard-roofed houses, turreted pseudo-Gothic Victorian houses with wooden "lace" festooned and carved on the porches, an old church which had been the site of a famous unsolved murder, where the writer Robert Blake had been found dead with the belfry reeking of some strange smell, and a weirdly shaped black stone in his hand. "Oh, there's decadence even in Arkham; it's just too old and too isolated," Colin told me. "There have been witch-cult murders and strange disappearances. If Arkham weren't so isolated, these things would have been as much of a *cause célèbre* as the Boston Strangler murders."

I shook my head in amazement. "And here I always thought of the country as being so wholesome, and crime as a special function of the big and wicked city."

"That's the favorite American myth," Colin said, turning into the restaurant after Brian's car. "In the city—the big city—there are police stations on every corner, welfare societies, and social workers. Last year when I was here, I heard of a family where the old man—a reeking old drunk—had six teenage daughters and every one of them had one or two children; guess who fathered them all? In any reasonably large town or city, the local welfare authorities and social agencies would have had all the girls in foster homes after the first one complained about her father abusing her; back out here, people pride themselves on minding their own business. 'We don't hold with interferin' between a man and his family,' they'll tell you with a straight face. The youngest girl was only about thirteen—hard to tell, and *she* didn't know, nobody ever bothered to tell her. And big as a house; baby due in a month."

"What did you do?" I asked.

"What *could* I do? I saw the baby delivered when the time came and made sure the social worker told the girl the facts of life. When I went out there again the middle girl—Ella May, I guess her name was—had been beaten with a harness strap and her back was all festered. I asked the old man what happened, and he told me he whipped her because she was laying up out behind the haystacks with one of the local boys and he didn't want none of his girls getting a name for being whores!"

I shuddered. "And Brian wants to devote his life to these people!"

Colin said seriously. "It sounds pretty awful, doesn't it? But every little bit he can do, helps. If he hadn't been there, that thirteen-year-old girl probably would have laid there and screamed herself hoarse for days when the baby came, while her teenage sisters did their ignorant best for her. Maybe it wouldn't make any difference in the cosmic purpose if she died in agony. Maybe it would be better in the long run if they *all* died; but while there's life there's hope that somebody may get through to them. He was the one who sent the district nurse around—she's a fine woman—and maybe after Joann talks to the girls, one or two of them will get up spunk enough to clout the old man with the frying pan next time he crawls into their beds—or to take those miserable kids and run away to Arkham, or Boston."

We went into the restaurant and met Brian there; I seized on a small point.

"Who is the district nurse?"

"Joann Winters? Well, she's a great girl; I lay her every Saturday, and I'll have to fit you in on my spare time—why Sara, you little green-eyed monster! You're jealous! Darling, Joann Winters is forty years old, she has three teenagers going to Miskatonic High School, and she's a devout member of the Baptist church, but she's a grand old girl, and if you're around me a lot you'll surely meet her. Her husband is the staff surgeon here at Arkham Hospital." While we waited for the waiter to seat us, and the men chatted, I thought with pleasure of the difference between Colin and Brian, and Matthew Hay. I could spend the rest of my life even in this isolated farm country with a man like Brian—I pulled myself up sharply; I'd known him just about twenty-four hours, and already I was thinking about spending the rest of my *life* with him?

All witches are promiscuous.

Oh, the hell with Matthew Hay, he was crazy—what was Colin's phrase?—*crazy as a crumpet*. What was his nutty logic?

All witches are promiscuous.

You are promiscuous.

Therefore you are a witch.

Even I could see the flaw in that logic. Anyhow, I wasn't promiscuous.

(What the hell do *you* call it, going to bed with two strange men inside twelve hours?)

Well, if Matthew Hay thought that because he could get me to lie down with him once I was going to accept his witch-nonsense and passively join up with his damned coven, or whatever he called it, he was going to get the surprise of his life. If he put his hands on me one more time I'd—again in Colin's phrase—clout him with Aunt Sara's frying pan! I was beginning to suspect that I'd have wanted Brian no matter where or how I met him. Maybe the night, the strangeness, my own sense of being lost and alone, the intimacy of Aunt Sara's big bedroom and vast four-poster, and even her strange perfume, had taken us by surprise and gotten us into bed a little faster than we might normally have landed there. But it would have happened anyhow, I'd bet. And what was the phrase that the students and hippies tossed around, back in Berkeley—*some of my best friendships began in bed?* It certainly seemed to have plummeted Brian and me into swift warm closeness. And I wanted it to last.

I loved Brian.

He was my own true love.

And to hell with Aunt Sara, and the witch-coven, and Matthew Hay. *Especially* Matthew Hay.

If a sneaking thought tormented me that it was easy to make such a resolve *away* from the old Latimer house, and might be harder to keep it when I was back there, I never allowed it to come up into my conscious mind. I sat back and waited for my love—I knew now that he was my love—to join us and the waiter to seat us for that shore dinner.

SEVEN

THE LIGHT IN THE GRAVEYARD

IT WAS A GREAT DINNER; THE INN LOOKED AS IF GEORGE WASHING-ton had slept there, and all of his men could have been fed off the same old china plates, under the same old crumbling copper lantern. But the food was marvelous, nothing frozen or canned or preserved; lobster we'd seen wriggling alive in a tank when we started our soup, salad greens so fresh they crackled, the kind which never made it into the city; the whole thing topped off with fresh peach pie covered with cream which had never seen a pasteurizing plant or a bottle. Afterward we dropped Colin off at the tourist cabin, and he left us; with me anticipating company in a day or two—I had known his assistant and partner in the bookstore, Claire Moffatt, while I was in California, and would be pleased to see her again.

I asked Colin, "Is Claire staying here?"

He actually blushed. "Oh, no, she's staying with some relatives in Madison Corners."

Brian, pulling out to take me home, said, "I'm free now for the evening; now, provided I call my answering service two or three times during the night, I'm all right. That's one thing about a country practice, it isn't a fifteen-hours-a-day business. I spend a lot of time on the road *between* patients—they're scattered all over hell's half acre—but numerically speaking, there aren't really so many of them. Maybe my colleagues were right and I'm just lazy, but I do like some time to live a life of my own anyway."

"I don't see anything wrong with that."

"And what about you, Sara? Are you terribly serious about a career, very much of a liberated woman? Or are you playing around with it, or what?"

"I'm not sure." I welcomed the opportunity to know Brian on a more personal level. "I'm sure that I want to accomplish something as an artist, even on a commercial level. If I can earn my living at it, so much the better, but even if I had to earn my living as something more mundane—a typist or a receptionist—I'd still keep on with my art, because it's part of what I *am,* part of what makes me a person. I go along with Women's Liberation this far, that I want to be something on my own, not just some man's pet or plaything. Or sex object."

He smiled and patted my knee. "Between you and me, Sara, a woman who's nothing *but* a sex object gets to be an awful damn bore. Let's face it, you can spend only so many hours in bed, and the woman who has nothing else on her mind is an awful drag the rest of the time. That far, I think most sane *men* go along with Women's Lib too. Everybody's tired of the walking womb, and between you and me, I think everybody except the half-wit population is sick to death of the walking breast-and-wiggling-hip female too. Oh, every man might enjoy an occasional bash on the mattress with one of the girls in the tight satin skirts, but for a long-term proposition, I'll take a girl with something else in her head except how-long-is-it-till-the-next-lay."

I felt warm and happy; so he too was thinking about long-term propositions?

Brian stopped at one of the larger local farms to call his answering service, and came back looking glum.

"I've got to stop and check a kid out down the road; his mother is making noises about strep throat. It's probably just one of the twenty-four-hour bugs, but—shall I take you home, or would you care to come along for the ride, and wait for me?"

"I'll ride along." There was no reason I had to be in a hurry to get back to the house, and dozens of reasons why I would rather not.

"We'll have to see about getting a telephone into the Latimer house, Sara. For two reasons. First, I'm *not* happy about having you completely isolated there. It was all very well for old Miss Latimer, she'd lived there all her life and by her own choice. But you're a young woman, and I'd feel better if you could yell for help even by wire. Second—well," he chuckled, "I expect—maybe I'd better say I *hope*—that I'll be spending some nights there, and a doctor can't really be out of earshot of his answering service for more than a couple of hours."

He reached out and squeezed my hand.

The rutted old road—more like a wagon lane than a country road—over which the car now bounced, made the Witch Hill Road look like a superhighway. "I hope you don't get stuck out here," I said, and Brian nodded. "One real danger of a country practice. It's really worst in the winter, or during the spring rains. Last winter I lost count of how many times some local farmer had to get out the tractor or even hitch up his mules, to haul me out of a snowbank or a mudhole. But it's still better than waiting for the triple-A tow trucks. The local farmers are all eager to keep me on the road—they never know when they, or their kids, might need the doctor next!"

It was getting dark when we drew up before an old isolated farmhouse, and Brian left me again in the car. The house was dark, a huge gambrel-roofed loom against the sky; on the other side a vast old barn rose dark and shadowy. In the swamp frogs croaked and a distant whippoorwill hooted with its strange cry. After a time, Brian came out and said, "The kid's not very sick but I've got to paint his throat and all they have is kerosene lamps. I have a battery-operated high-powered light in my bag; you want to come in and hold it for me?"

"Sure." I climbed out and followed Brian into the dark, lamp-lit old kitchen and through the back bedroom where a very small, tow-headed boy sat apprehensively on the edge of the bed.

"Hold the light here, Sara, so I can see down his throat. Okay, Sonny, open up, this won't hurt; just going to check your tonsils." He swabbed the throat swiftly by the strong light. "Okay, that's it; here, I've got a big red lollipop for you. Now, Mrs. Fairfield, I want you to keep him in bed another day, and if his fever goes up again, give him one of these tablets every four hours, but I think he'll be fine. If any of the other kids get a sore throat, though, you'd better give me a call and we'll take a culture."

I lowered the light, which had blinded me, and realized that the farm woman—a tall, wiry young woman in a print blouse and man's dungarees—was staring at me, her mouth slightly open. As my eyes rested on her, she drew back, still staring warily at me.

She said, "How come you're bringing ole Miss Sarie round to overlook my young 'uns? Doctor, that 'air woman's a witch!" She advanced on me, and for a moment I actually thought she would strike me. "Here, you, get along out of this, I don't want the likes of you in my house!"

Brian stepped between us. He said, "Look here, Mrs. Fairfield—Annie—this is nonsense. In the first place, there are no such things as witches." *Well,* I thought, *that's going too far.* "In the second place, Miss Latimer has just come here from New York. She certainly is no one you have ever seen before."

"Doctor," Annie Fairfield said, "you may know a lot about curin' and medicine, but I lived here all my life, and I know what I know, and I know ole Miss Sarie when I see her. If she's no witch, how come she's the livin' spit and image of that 'air ole witch up on Witch Hill Road?"

I said firmly, "Miss Sara Latimer was my great-aunt and she's been dead for years, Mrs. Fairfield. I never knew her, or even saw her."

Annie Fairfield turned her back on me. She said, "Doctor, you know and I know that the Latimer witches, they don't die, they just come back, lookin' just like before. Now maybe she can fool you, but she cain't fool me! So you take her along out of this, and don't you bring her back here no more, Doctor. I got my young 'uns to think of."

Brian said disgustedly, "Annie, you're a fool," and took up his bag, escorting me to the car. Outside, he noted that the kitchen curtain was pulled back and the woman was staring balefully at me through the darkening pane. He slammed the car door and backed it around so energetically that he nearly rammed into a haystack.

"Damn fool girl!" he muttered. "Sara—darling, I'm sorry about that. I thought Annie Fairfield had more sense; I went to school with her. I hope you don't have to face this all over the countryside!"

"You don't think I care what they say?" But I was more shaken than I cared to let Brian know; it was tiresome to be mistaken for my Aunt Sara at every turn. It would be hard to make myself any sort of life in this countryside if everywhere I went I must fight her reputation as a witch. *And according to Matthew Hay, the reputation was well-deserved.*

"I guess I ought to be glad they can't hang witches any more, or I'd get a fast trip to Witch Hill on my own," I wisecracked. "Brian, forget it; the woman is demented or ignorant. But I forgot—it won't do *your* reputation in the countryside any good to be seen all around with the local witch."

Brian stopped the car short in the narrow road and put out his hands to me. He said quietly, "Get one thing straight now, Sara. I earn my living as a doctor here, but I don't owe them anything. They need me; I don't need them. And if they think their opinion is going to change my ways, or have any effect on my choice when it comes to women, they're just going to have to learn different."

I came into his arms, reveling in the mixture of gentleness and masterfulness. He kissed me, long and hard, and his hands moved on my breasts; but then he drew back.

"Not here," he said quietly, "I'm not really an impulsive person, Sara, and I want it to be something we both want, this time, not something I rush you into when you're lonely and off base. Let me take you home now, and if you want me to stay—"

"I do," I said swiftly, "but don't take me home, Brian. This time I want it to be—somewhere else. Not under the—the influence of that damned house And that damned room!" *So I can be sure it's myself—not Aunt Sara!*

He turned the key in the ignition, and said, "I think you're letting the place get on your nerves, Sara, but I can understand how you feel. Anyway, I really can't spend another night out of earshot of the telephone. Cousin James—" he hesitated. "There isn't a hotel this side of Arkham, or I'd take you there. But Cousin James is as deaf as the proverbial post, and there's no one else to object; will you come and spend the night—or most of it, anyway—at my place?"

I felt my excitement rising as we drove through the silent countryside and into the village of Madison Corners. This time it was not the baleful influence of the witch-house or Aunt Sara's erotic perfumes. This time it was what Brian and I wanted, just our two selves.

He drew up before a house with low lights burning in two or three rooms. He said, "Cousin James is tucked up before the TV set in his own room; I'll warn him that I'm in and he can turn his telephone off—as I said, he's deaf and when it's his night to answer, he turns the bell way up. My quarters are upstairs and he won't know whether I've got a whole harem up here."

The house was nearly as old, and nearly as much of an architectural monstrosity, as the Latimer house; but inside it smelled warm and good, smells of fresh cooking, soap, furniture polish and a faint medical smell—ether or disinfectant, perhaps—from a half-opened office door giving on the front hall. Brian left me briefly in the warm-wood lights of the hall, and I heard his voice raised in the character-istic shout of someone talking to the deaf, then he came back, smil-ing. He said, "Cousin James does turn off his hearing aid, nights, and forgets about it! And he can't even hear me tell him to turn it up! I even have to shake him to get his attention!"

His arm tightened around my shoulders as we went up the stairs. He opened a door; inside his room was clean and spacious, with an old brass bed covered with a patchwork quilt in bright colors, almost a museum piece of needlecraft. Brian lifted the telephone by his bed and said, "No calls for an hour or so unless it's a major emergency; I'll check back at—well, it's eleven-thirty now; I'll call in about one in the morn-ing." Then he locked the door and came to take me in his arms. He kissed me, long and hard, then tugged gently at my sweater.

"I can't wait, green-eyes."

I kicked off my sandals, unbuttoning my skirt in one swift mo-tion. When I stood naked on the old-fashioned rag rug, he came and seized me.

"You're even more beautiful by electric light! You'll never need soft lights to look sexy!" He drew me toward the bed, switching on a bed-lamp above; but as he caressed me, he stopped, staring in horror at my body. I followed his eyes, and saw the darkening bruises there, left by Matthew Hay's hard hands.

"My God!" he gasped. "Did I do that to you?"

What could I say? My mind spun wildly, and I felt sick and dizzy. Finally I said, "I bruise so easily, darling!" and I felt false and ashamed.

His fingers moved, with infinite tenderness, on the ugly darken-ing patches. He said, "I'll handle you like a piece of precious china this time, love, I promise. I wouldn't hurt you for anything." He still looked faintly puzzled. "I never realized I was that rough. Sara, if you bruise as easily as all that, you may be anemic—perhaps I ought to give you a checkup."

I could hardly bear my guilt, and it made me brusque. "I'm not your patient, Doctor Standish—not now, anyhow. And if I were— this is neither the time or the place—"

"Right you are." He leaned down and kissed each dark bruise. His mouth felt warm and his breath tickled my nipples to hardness. I shut my eyes so that I would reveal nothing. I hated myself. At that moment I wanted desperately to pour out the truth, how Matthew Hay had caught me unawares and taken me on his foul altar. But I was still not sure of him; I felt I could not bear it, to see his eyes darken with suspicion, distrust, cynicism. At best, he would be hurt and jealous. I pulled him down to me, my hands groping at his loins, my mouth closing over his in a wild, strangling kiss.

"Brian—Brian—I want you, I want you!"

His mouth met mine, tongue probing in a long kiss, then he raised himself on his two hands and looked down at me, smiling and amused.

"Don't be in a hurry, love. We've got all night. Let's make it last."

His mouth moved sensuously over my naked body, kissing my breasts, my belly, my thighs, the creases of my knees. He picked up my feet, nibbled briefly at each toe in turn. When he finally came into me, it was with infinite gentleness, moving for a long time, slowly, imperceptibly, with long pauses and lengthy kisses, until I moaned with need and growing hunger. We moved together more and more closely, exploding with climax at almost the same instant.

We lay together, cuddled close, for a long time afterward, talking quietly, moving now and again to quiet caresses; later we went down and made coffee in the deserted kitchen, and after checking with the answering service, he took me home. He stood holding me, for a long time, in the shadow of the doorway, but finally let me go.

"If I come in, I'll take you upstairs again," he muttered regretfully, "and it *is* my night to be on call." He kissed me hard enough to leave a mark. "Sleep well, darling. Dream of me. I'll see you tomorrow."

But when his car had driven away and the dank darkness of the old house has closed around me again, the elation and joy of the evening ebbed slowly away from me again, leaving me empty, drained, and weak. I found the flashlight—I didn't have the energy to cope with the damned kerosene lamps at this hour—and went upstairs. Barnabas emerged from a corner, his wicked yellow eyes gleaming like hot coals as he stalked upstairs, his tail waving, and jumped up before me on Aunt Sara's bed. I ran down again at the last minute to make certain the door was bolted, and as I checked the back door, a strange sound made me stop short, my heart pounding in my chest:

It sounded like a step, a dragging sound, but where? In the house? In the graveyard? I ran swiftly up again, barking my shins on some unexpected piece of furniture in the hall, and inside Aunt Sara's room, went to the window, turning out the flashlight and flattening my face against the glass.

The moon was low in the sky, a reddish and inflamed half-disk surrounded by thin, flaky clouds. In the darkness of the graveyard, the dilapidated marble mounds showed whitish, leaning every which way against their black background. Then one of the whitish forms seemed to move, to be blotted out—or had a dark, invisible form moved past it in the dimness? I held my breath; yes, there was another movement and the faint flicker of a dim light. Was someone carrying a candle in the graveyard? Was Matthew Hay watching me from out there? Or was he at his disgusting rites somewhere in the place? My door was bolted inside; I should worry! Let him prowl around the graveyard and make love to the corpses if it suited his lunatic fancy!

I told myself to go to bed and forget about him, but I remained at the window, stiff and paralyzed. After a long interval, a second light joined the flickering first, both so dim that I found myself wondering if I had really seen them or imagined them. Could they be the dim phosphorescence which is sometimes found on old trees and rotten logs? Could not these will-o'-the-wisp lights appear on the damp sides of old marble slabs?

The lights were gone. I finally dragged myself away from the window, fell into Aunt Sara's four-poster and hauled a pillow over my head. As I drifted off to sleep it occurred to me to wonder if Matthew Hay had come to pick herbs in the garden. Weren't there herbs which had to be picked in the last quarter of the moon, or something? Did that mean by moonlight, or simply when the moon was in its last quarter, night or day?

And who cared, anyhow? Not me. I reached in the dark for Barnabas, whose thick purr was steady and reassuring, and fell asleep stroking his silky head.

EIGHT

WITCH SISTER

I KNEW I WAS DREAMING. STILL, THERE WAS AN EERIE REALISM IN it, as if it were more memory than dream . . .

I stood atop the hill, below the blasted oak, and heard voices howling for my blood.

"Sara Latimer!"

"Kill her! Hang the witch!"

"Drown her! Duck her!"

I was wearing a long serge gown which buttoned tight over my breasts, a white kerchief modestly folded at my neck, trailing full skirt. The two men who stood over me, their hands hard on my arms, were dressed in dark suits and wide collars and tall hats. *They look like the Pilgrim Fathers in the school Thanksgiving play!*

I tried desperately to catch their eyes. Jethro Hay refused to look at me and I felt his hands tremble. Well he might! So many times we had lain together on the hillside, our naked bodies throbbing together, the night-winds playing over us. And now he tried to play the proper man! *Damned hypocrite!*

I looked down, with contempt, on the shouting, screaming

women below. Was it my fault if their men would rather sleep with me than with any of that mealy-mouthed, tight-arsed crew? I threw back my head and laughed, the loud shrill laughter they hated me for.

"Jethro, does thee still pretend to have cramp in the bowels till after Ruth is asleep, so that thy long-nosed wife will not know thee wants no one but me in thy bed?"

His face contorted with rage.

"Silence, accursed devil-spawn!" He struck me, hard, across the face; I felt blood break from my lip.

I laughed up at the solemn face of the other man. "Has thee forgotten, Preserved, that thee begged me—oh, and on a solemn fast-day, too—to walk in the orchard, and that thee did snatch off my kerchief and swear my breasts were like ripe plums?"

Preserved Whitfield did not look at me. He ripped my kerchief from my neck with a rough gesture and jerking my head harshly back, crammed one end in my mouth and gagged me. "The words of the harlot shall not be heard!"

With one hand, Jethro ripped my long hair down; jerked at the buttons on my frock so that I stood naked to the waist. The cries of the crowd grew louder.

"Kill her! Burn her!"

"Suffer not a witch to live!"

"She has bewitched our husbands, our sons!"

"Stone her! Stone her!"

A rotten-ripe fruit squished against my face. I began to struggle and scream; pain raked down my cheek, and I woke—

Barnabas was squatting on my chest, striking gently at my cheek with one unsheathed claw. I shook my head blearily, coming free of nightmare. Had I been dreaming of Sara the First again—really the first, the one who was hanged as a witch? Had there ever been any witches back in those days, or was this the excuse a superstitious, sex-starved populace used to get rid of any misfit? Any girl brighter and more intelligent than most, who attracted attention which those re-pressed, sex-hating men could not dare to admit was simply desire, and had to call witchcraft or a demon-spell? I knew they had feared ugly old women who knew a bit too much of herbs or lore, who per-haps kept strange pets, who were, perhaps, a bit simple and talked to themselves or to their odd roosters or jackdaws or cats.

But—the witch-covens, the organized religion? Was this devil-worship? Or had some misfits among the Pilgrim Fathers brought along a small enclave of a worship older than Christianity, the fertility-religions which were there before the churches came along, and which Christianity tried to mop up and absorb?

I knew only one way to find out—ask Matthew Hay—and I'd be *damned* if I'd have anything to do with that man again! (Yes, I thought, I probably would. Be damned, that is.)

I washed my face, cooked myself an ample breakfast, fed Barnabas—who abandoned the mouse he had caught for a can of Puss'N'Boots—and spent the morning cheerfully painting in the studio. I felt more like myself than I'd felt since coming to this dis-aster of a house.

I worked most of the morning, stopping around noon to fix a tuna fish sandwich which I shared with Barnabas, in a hurry to get back to my easel while things were going so well. In the early after-noon—I was not sure of the time—the ancient bell jangled. I was torn between irritation at being interrupted while working, and anticipation that Brian had managed to get away; I ran downstairs, careless that I was in blue jeans and an old blouse, my hair tousled. I opened the door and saw Matthew Hay, standing on the porch with a woman I had never seen before.

My heart sank and my spirits disappeared. My welcoming smile must have gone with it, for Matthew asked:

"Have we come at the wrong time, Sara?"

"Well, I *was* working."

"I imagine this is more important," Matthew said. "We'd better come in; I'd rather not let the neighbors see us all standing here on the porch. They aren't all—of us."

Neighbors? Nobody overlooked the old house except the inhabitants of the old graveyard—and a couple of placid cows. But that was New England for you. The way Matthew spoke, we could have been overlooked by forty houses, each with a gossipy old lady at every window. Oh, hell, maybe we were. I said, resigned, "Come in."

Without further by-your-leave, they came inside and went directly into the old parlor as if they knew their way. Matthew came over and took my hand intimately. He said, "Sara my dear, I want you to know Tabitha Whitfield. Again."

Tabitha was small and slender, nicely rounded with a slim waist and small pointed breasts for which she obviously needed—and wore—no bra. Because of her fluffy blonde hair and small kitten-round face, I thought at first that she was a young girl, not much out of her teens; then a sharper look at the tell-tale spots, her thin neck, her hands, betrayed that she was at least thirty and might have been older. Nevertheless she was surprisingly pretty, with an air of bright sensuality.

I waited until they were seated, but stood away myself, aloof and very much on my guard. I did not trust Matthew Hay, and I wasn't going to let him get any advantage of me again.

Not ever. Not in this life—or the next, if I could help it.

It was Tabitha who spoke first. Looking back and forth from me to the painted face of Aunt Sara on the wall, she said, "Yes, a remarkable likeness. It's really amazing. But I'm not sure it means what you think it does, Matt."

Matthew said, "I'm afraid you must leave that to me, Tabitha."

A strong spark of antagonism seemed to flash between them—and yet there was an undercurrent of intimacy, of knowing just where to look for the other's weaknesses which comes only from long knowledge. I knew, as if I'd been told in words, that these two were lovers—no; it was too difficult to think of love where Matthew Hay was concerned. But they were sexual partners of long standing and knew one another well. And I was astonished to find myself feeling a surge of possessive jealousy. *How dare she usurp my place! Matthew was mine to do with as I chose, and had been for these last twenty years! Or more accurately, the last seven hundred! He might amuse himself when I gave him leave, but he should learn who was his true mistress!*

I shook my head as if to clear it of fuzz. What on earth was the matter with me? It was this room. It so definitely belonged to Aunt Sara and not to me.

Could I even think my own thoughts in it?

Matthew said, "I neglected to ask you yesterday, Sara. Have you any particular birthmarks?"

Tabitha said, with a faintly jeering note, "Do you mean you didn't investigate while you had her naked?"

"Look here," I said, outraged, "you can't come here and talk like that—"

"Oh, Sara," Matthew said, almost laughing, "there is a great deal to accomplish; please don't try to obstruct us by this nonsense. I know it often suits you to play games. But the modesty game doesn't suit you, especially after yesterday, and it's a waste of time. Try it on with people who aren't in the know, like your young doctor. Amuse yourself all you like, but don't play games with *us.*" He walked over, calmly unbuttoned my blouse and drew it down over my shoulder, laying his finger on the small brown mole at the edge where my armpit joined my back. "See, Tabitha, now are you convinced?"

I jerked at my blouse. "Don't I have anything to say—"

"I asked you not to play games, Sara. We haven't the time. After all, the Esbat is at sunset tomorrow, and there is much we must accomplish by then. Your memories should be back by that time, but if you haven't recovered them all, it doesn't matter; this will only be a ceremony of welcome. I brought Tibby here—wait a minute. First of all; do you recognize her?"

"Recognize her? I never saw her before in my life," I said. I felt like Alice at the Mad Hatter's Tea Party, with meaningless questions to which my answers would make no real difference. "Why should I?"

"You never saw her before, you say? That complicates things," Matthew said. "What you mean, of course, is that you never saw her before in *this* life. Well, Tibby has been one of us for centuries, even as you have, Sara."

They were completely mad. Insane. Crazy as a crumpet—a couple of crumpets. But what could I do?

I stood there buttoning my blouse with fingers that trembled insanely. I had walked into a nightmare. *Oh, Brian, Brian!* I tried to summon up the memory of his face, his sane, normal voice, but memory failed. I couldn't even remember for a moment what he looked like.

Matthew said, "Tibby is one of your sisters in the coven—she has been serving as our leader. But of course, now that you have returned, she will be happy to yield her place to you."

I caught Tibby's glance, and thought, *in a pig's eye*. Matthew might know a lot about witchcraft, but he didn't know a damned thing about *women*, and witch or no, Tibby was a woman. She was smiling sweetly, but underneath it she was a blaze of jealousy and resentment.

Was it Matthew she wanted—or power among the witches?

I didn't know and I didn't really care, but I might be able to use it somehow.

"Tibby will teach you everything which you may have forgotten in your early years in this rebirth," Matthew said, "those things which only a woman may teach another. I hope you will be close again, and love one another as sisters. I'll leave you now to get acquainted—or reacquainted."

He leaned over and kissed me in a smug assumption of intimacy, touched Tibby lightly on the cheek and turned to go. I said, "Matthew, wait a minute."

He inclined his head, listening.

"You say I'm Sara Latimer reborn. Now listen! Aunt Sara only died seven years ago and I'm twenty-three years old! You can't have it both ways, can you?"

Tibby said, "I told you she didn't understand. You're making a mistake, Matthew."

He turned his glittering eyes on me. "The witch, Sara Latimer, never dies. She returns again and again; when one body dies, her immortal part—her soul, if you choose—takes refuge in the body of another woman of her family. Your family, the Latimers, is one of the old witch-lines, and again and again, in every couple of generations, a girl will be born who has the marks of the witch. Like you, Sara. She will be normal—although she will have certain inborn powers. But when her predecessor dies, the soul of the witch enters her and possesses her. And when this happens, she quickly assumes the memory, the position—and all the powers—of the witch. This has now happened to you, Sara. You may not fully know it yet—you may not be entirely aware of your powers and your past. But you proved it to me yesterday, before the altar. The rest of your memories will soon return—and you will be one with us again, through all the ages, through life, and death, and after."

He turned and walked out, leaving me standing, appalled.

Tibby rose and came toward me. She said, more gently than usual, "You look frightened, Sara. I've been part of this so long, and so has Matthew, we tend to forget how strange it all may seem to an outsider. What can I say or do that will help?"

She put her arms around me. I leaned back to look at her and said, "I'd have sworn there was no love lost between you and Sara."

"There isn't," she said, "but I take my oath seriously too, and I'm sworn to treat you as a sister in the coven. Besides, you look sort of young and lost." She stroked my cheek. "There's nothing to be frightened of. Matthew is formidable, but it's all part of being what he is. If I know him, he jumped you without warning and probably scared you half to death."

"Not really," I said honestly, "to tell the truth I think I was half expecting it."

"But he's like most men," Tibby said with a trace of contempt. "Oh, don't get me wrong, I'm nuts about him, but like all other men, he thinks his big cock can solve anything." She must have seen my startled look, for she said, with a certain diffidence, "Sorry; I don't mean to be coarse. But Matt can be a damn fool, too."

Her hands lingered, with a curious and disquieting intimacy, on my breasts; I looked down in surprise and she took them away, without haste. She said, "Do you mind? I was simply admiring them."

I felt the same odd lack of surprise I had felt when Matthew made sexual advances. *All witches are promiscuous and take their pleasure easily, without pretensions.* "Are you a lesbian?"

"Only from time to time," she said. "I wouldn't mind, if you wanted it, or needed it. We could probably give each other some pleasure."

I laughed, in some embarrassment. Her matter-of-fact acceptance made me feel naive, even though I had moved in relatively sophisticated circles. Or was this simply decadence gone so far as to be completely shameless? I said, "Not now, thanks." I tried to load the words with irony, but they came out as matter-of-fact as Tibby's own, and I felt myself wondering, *why make such a fuss about anything so simple!*

I said, "Do witches drink coffee? Or tea?"

She chuckled. "If you haven't any beer, tea is fine. I think that's a good idea. Sharing food or drink is the fastest—well, it's a beginning. When Matthew brought me here I was prepared for you to hate me."

"I guess I don't hate people very easily," I said. I led the way into the kitchen and put the kettle over to boil. "I use teabags; do you mind? I know gourmet philosophy would be outraged, but I can't cope with those messy little leaves all over everything, and I hate to get them loose in my cup."

"Gourmet philosophy be damned," Tibby agreed, "I use them too. I suspect witches were the original Women's Lib; they were the ones who refused to be martyrs to somebody's notion of what a woman ought to be and do. My father is the sort of bastard who believed that the whole duty of women was to make some man happy. My mother scrubbed the floor with lye, on her hands and knees, every day of her life, just because he didn't like linoleum in the kitchen. She used to protest once in a while, that she didn't have time— maybe in haying or threshing season—and he'd jump up and down and yell 'Jumping Jiminy, woman, what's your time *for?*' When she died, I went and took my egg money and laid down linoleum in the kitchen, and my father tried to raise hell, and I said, 'Take that lino out of here and you'll scrub your own damn floor, or live with it dirty!' He left it there. I guess he decided the linoleum was a lesser evil."

The teakettle whistled; I poured it over the bags in the pot. "Want to hand me a couple of cups out of the cabinet? Thanks." Tibby sat down at the kitchen table, taking the full cup I handed her.

"Sugar? Milk?"

"As it comes, thanks." She sipped.

"Tibby," I said, "tell me something straight out, without faking it, and without pulling any punches. Are you serious about all this witch stuff, or is it a game you play?"

She looked squarely across the table at me. She said, "I won't con you. Sometimes I think it's one, and sometimes I think it's the other. There are times when I believe it all completely, and I'm wrapped up in it; then it seems that it's my life. And there are times when I wonder if I'm kidding myself and playing along because it's Matt's game and—in case you haven't guessed—I'm crazy about him."

"I'd guessed," I said. "But how does a sane person *get* involved in something with such—such peculiar beliefs? How do people get into it at all?"

"You've never lived in New England's back country," she said. "Let's face it, what else is there for a woman here? I suspect witchcraft got its hold in Salem, and other places, because it was the only way women could be *people*—not just sleeping partners, slaves and child-bearers for some damn man, some ignorant brute. There weren't enough intelligent, reasonable, liberated men to go round. A woman who didn't marry was socially dead, and a woman who did was almost literally her husband's slave. I read somewhere that Massachusetts and Connecticut are the only states which still had stringent laws against birth control, even with a doctor's permission, till *Roe versus Wade* overthrew them all at once."

I could see how the repressive world of old New England had made women rebellious—and was it any wonder if they used their husband's own superstitious fears against them?

She said, "I can imagine how a woman who had had seven children in six years—and believe me, even in this day and age there are plenty of them—might want her husband impotent for a while!"

"Do you think it's all a sex-cult then? Born out of boredom and repression?"

"There are times when I think so," Tibby repeated. "And there are times when I feel that I have proof that it's more than that. After you've been to a few of the Esbats, you'll know what I mean. No matter how flip I talk about it, I'm convinced enough that I'd never dare to try and get out of it."

I suddenly realized I liked Tibby, and felt sorry for her. Life couldn't be any picnic for an intelligent feminist in the world she had grown up in. I remembered the story of the brutish old farmer with the six teenage daughters he'd made into his own private harem. It was only a difference in degree, not in kind of abuse, I suspected. Once you begin to think of wives and daughters as slaves, chattels created for your convenience, why should you stop at anything? Her father may not have abused her sexually, but he had certainly not allowed her any real freedom to build up some decent life which would use all of her intellect and capabilities. I said, "Why didn't you ever leave home, Tibby? Girls like you are getting good jobs in every big city in the country."

She shrugged. "My people were convinced that college for a woman was a waste—I'd just want to get married. My mother could no more imagine a woman not wanting to get married, than she could imagine—well, than she could imagine my screwing Matt Hay in broad daylight on his altar. Only I could do the one in secret, and not the other. So here I am at thirty-two, no education, no talent, no training; if I left home I'd spend my life working as a waitress somewhere or sacking laundry. So I stay here and keep house for the old man, and when he dies, well, I'll have a home without having to marry some local bastard to get it. But do you blame me if witchcraft has become a way of life?"

"How did you get into it?" I poured her more tea.

"I have your Aunt Sara to thank for that. Oh, she was a dreadful woman in many ways, but she was intelligent. She loaned me books—we had nothing but the family Bible and the almanac. She helped me start thinking for myself; then she brought me into the coven. I was only seventeen when she gave me the nerve to stop going to church—Pa belongs to some ghastly hellfire-and-damnation sect. I owe her a lot. She was a holy terror, but I suppose in some crazy way I loved her, because she taught me to be free, and to enjoy life and live it fully, even in a backwoods hellhole like this." She reached across the table and took my hand. "After she died, I felt I had a right to her place in the coven. This is why I resented you coming back."

I returned the pressure of her hand. "Tibby," I said, "believe me, I'm no threat to you. I don't believe that I'm Sara Latimer—or rather, I'm not the Latimer witch reborn, or returned. I'm not interested in leading the coven. I don't want any part of it. As for Matthew, he's all yours. I wouldn't have him as a gift tied up with pink ribbons."

Her eyes met mine, level and unhappy. "You say that now," she said, "but what about later? If your witch-memory returns? Haven't you had flashes of it? Didn't Matt say that you knew more of the business of the cult than any outsider could ever know?"

"I can't explain that," I said. For instance, what was all that about knives? And names? I remembered that in anthropology, to know a person's true name was to have great power against him; and in some preliterate societies, to take a person's photograph was to own—or steal—his soul. Did this have something to do with that threat—I know your name? I dismissed that for now. "Any more than I can explain why I—why I had sex with Matthew. Believe me, I didn't want to, and didn't intend to. But couldn't it be simple suggestion?"

Tibby thought about it. She said, "Maybe if you'd never come here, you never would have had any—any impetus to be a witch. But you *did* come here. And now it *has* been stimulated in you. And you *did* respond to Matt, and you *did* discover that you knew about the cult. What will happen after you've been to a couple of the Esbats, and after you've used the unguent a few times?"

I did not answer at once, for a curious revulsion of feeling had come over me. I stood erect, looking down on this woman who had dared to usurp my place in the coven, even thought she could take my place with Matthew and use him for her own purposes. I saw Tabitha with a strange double sight, as if I were still sitting across from her at the table, and as if I were standing, looming over her. I rapped out, "By what right do you question me, Tabitha Whitfield? *I know your name!*"

Names again; yet it had come from me with absolute surety. *I must certainly have been going nuts.* She backed away, her chair suddenly crashing to the floor; her teacup tipped and splattered cooling tea all over the white oilcloth on the table. "Sara," she whispered.

"That was the wrong question," I said remotely. I was still oddly divided inside. "I wish you hadn't asked me that, Tibby. I'm not sure what happened."

She shook her head. "I'm confused. It's you and still, somehow, not you."

In a wave of anguish I realized that it had happened again, the curious unrealness that had overcome me, that had stampeded Brian into my bed, thrown me naked before an alien altar with Matthew, now might alienate a girl who in a few moments of strangely honest, intimate talk had come to feel like a close friend of long standing. I covered my face with my hands.

"Oh, God, I hate this place," I burst out, "I don't know what's happening to me! Tibby, Tibby, what the hell shall I do? If I stay here it'll get me, and I have no place to go!"

Tibby came around the table to me. She put her arms round me as she had done before. She said, "Whichever way it goes, Sara, remember I love you and I want to be your friend."

"Perhaps if I stayed away from all of it—if I refused to attend the what-is-it?, Sabbat, Esbat or whatever, if I threw away all of Aunt Sara's things—"

She shook her head. "I don't think you can do that now. Maybe you could have once. I'm afraid it's gone too far. And anyhow, Matthew would be very angry. I don't know about you, but I can't stand up against him." She smiled shakily. "Neither can you—this way. And if you're in your witch-self, you *can*—I've seen you—but you don't want to get away then."

It seemed fairly hopeless. With shaking hands I picked up my teacup and drank the cold brew. Tibby said, "I promised Matthew I'd go over everything with you—the use of the unguent, the other potions—"

"No!" I said frantically. "No! I don't want any part of it—"

"But I promised Matthew—"

Stalemate; we stood, looking stubbornly at one another, until there was a loud, peremptory knock on the back door. Tibby said, "I'd rather the neighbors didn't see me here," and stepped back. Slowly, with frozen feet, I went to the door.

A heavy-set, overalled, slouching figure stood there, an unshaven middle-aged man whom, after a moment, I recognized as old Jeb from the night I had gotten off the Arkham-Innsmouth bus. He touched his dirty forelock in a sort of salute.

"I brought your bottled gas, ma'am. Storekeeper up to Madison Corners told me you'd be needing it and I better bring it by and connect it up for you."

Brought abruptly back to mundane facts by this, I nodded, and he said, "I'll get my wrench and fix it for you on the platform, right here outside the kitchen window. No need to pay me now, storekeeper will bill you the way he always billed the Latimers, come the first of every month."

He went off toward his truck, and I realized that there was at least one advantage to belonging to a known local family—my credit was good! This might mean that my slender savings would last a little longer than I had expected, probably carry me through until I was paid for my book, without even arranging to sell some of Aunt Sara's antiques.

Tibby murmured, "You'd better go out and watch him hook it up, hadn't you? Then you'll know where it goes."

I supposed she was right. I didn't know much about country living—in the city I'd taken the supply of gas, heat, electricity for granted—but I supposed here I should know, so I went outside and watched as the hulking figure tipped the big metal cylinder off his truck, trundled it on its wheeled dolly to the platform outside the kitchen window, where a small copper tube ran in through a hole cut in the wall, and deftly tipped away the old cylinder.

"Ayeh, this one's near about empty, prob'ly give out before you could bile an egg," he said. "That'll last you about a month, less'n you bake your own bread, and keep the oven going a lot."

I watched him fumbling with the copper nozzle. His hands were huge, stubby, curiously deft. With that strange double awareness, I wondered what they would feel like on my breasts, my naked body.

He was so enormous, so animal, so much of the earth. To lie in his arms would be like sinking deep into the earth, becoming one with the elemental forces of ancient sub-human strength. . . . I felt his eyes, small and leering, rest on me, move over me with a strange assumption of intimacy. *Had he read my thoughts?*

He said, "Now you're back, you want me to come upstairs with you like always, Miss Sara?"

Oh, God, was he one of them too? No, this was too much. *All witches are promiscuous.* I felt myself wriggling in eager anticipation of his big hands on me, ripping off my dress . . .

No, damn it! I was still in command of myself. I didn't have to let myself be stampeded into anything more. I said flatly, "I don't know what you mean. There's nothing for you to do in the house," and saw his face change back to the puzzled look of respect. He said, "Jus' as you like, Miss Sara," lurched back to his truck and I stood and watched it rattle away down the hill.

I went inside feeling a curious elation. For the first time since coming here I had won out, my real self had asserted what I really wanted to do; I had not been forced to behave in that strange way so alien to me. I looked for Tibby in the kitchen, longing to tell her what had happened, but she was nowhere in sight, and I wondered if she had simply slipped out the front door and run home. If she was one of the Whitfields, her family home was down the road toward the corner where the Arkham bus passed, and—yes; it was the Whitfield farm where Matthew had said I could buy milk, eggs, garden stuff. This would be a little awkward if I chose to have nothing to do with the witch-coven; how could I deal with them?

I went slowly upstairs. In Aunt Sara's big bedroom, Tibby was waiting. She had taken off her shoes and was sitting, barefoot, on the bench before the dressing table. She said, "Why didn't you bring him upstairs? He's man enough for both of us." At my look of shock and horror, she said impatiently, "Oh, Sara, don't be foolish. All right, all

right, I won't rush things, then. The Esbat is tomorrow night, anyway, and I can wait."

She came and stood by me. "I'm sorry, I—you've got to understand what it's like for me. I have every reason to expect you to behave like one of *us,* and you keep throwing me off balance. I hate to
keep apologizing, after all."

"I'm not angry," I said. "I don't know why, but I'm not."

She bent over the dressing table. She said, "I see you found the
unguent of Venus. It's not a very serious thing, but it's fun to play
with." She opened the little porcelain jar and the strange, erotic,
compelling scent stole out.

Made uneasy by the scent, I moved a little away. I said, "Is this
the unguent you said I'd be using before the—" I fumbled for her
phrase, "before the witch-memory came back?"

She looked at me sharply. "No," she said, "this is a game. Do
you mean to tell me that you've forgotten what the true witch-
unguent—*the* unguent—is, and what it can do?"

"Forgotten, or never knew. And don't really give a damn," I said.
Tibby was absent-mindedly rubbing the stuff in the porcelain jar on
her wrists and temples. "Do you really want to play around with that
stuff, Tibby? I got the impression the other night that it could be reasonably dangerous." The smell was intoxicating, with a curious sting
at the root of my nose and an odd surge of blurred memories and confused thoughts. Tibby laughed up at me in the mirror.

"Dangerous? Not this. The real unguent—get an overdose of
that and you'll have one hell of a bad trip; get a *real* overdose and
you'll be poisoned, though nobody's died of it here in years. But
there's nothing in this to hurt anyone; it's just for fun. Here, why
don't you join me? It might be the best way after all, to help you.
Maybe Matthew meant this."

I felt, again, that odd overlay of emotions, memories, fantasies.
Tibby, her face wavering in the mirror, seemed at once much younger

and much older. The scent of the erotic ointment was like a visible miasma in the room. Slowly, indecisively, I reached down, took a fingertip-worth of the greenish paste and touched it to my throat.

"Here, let me," Tibby said. She opened the buttons on my blouse; the paste felt cold, briefly stinging, then pleasant on my bare breasts. Her hands lingered, gentle, intimate, touching one of the bruises which still darkened them. "Matt is too damn rough, but who cares? I like it that way. Look." She pulled her own T-shirt off in one swift move and I saw reddish bite-marks on her shoulder. I reached out the tip of one finger and touched them, gently, with a strange, not unpleasant thrill of horror.

"Too bad Matt didn't stay," she said, "but never mind, we can manage well enough without him."

She was kicking off her heavy, boyish jeans; she wore no panties under them, and naked, she looked very slender and frail, almost childlike, so vulnerable that I was moved to an irrational sense of compassion. But her wicked grin gave the lie to anything young or innocent about her; her eyes, slanting up through her disheveled hair, were wide and gleaming with something of the same knowing evil as Barnabas's eyes.

The erotic unguent was beginning to work on me, too. It seemed as if all the sensation in my body was concentrated in the tips of my fingers, which still lightly explored Tibby's breasts. She laughed, a wild high laugh like the cry of a seabird, and pulled me down beside her on the big bed.

Of all the strange events of that strange summer in the old Latimer house, the one I remember with the strangest emotion is that hour I spent with Tibby on Aunt Sara's enormous four-poster, the strange perfume around us making us both wild and lazily sensual by turns, the room filled with soft wavering sunlight which seemed from time to time to pause and dance and quiver with my own quivering nerves. For everything else that happened that summer, there seems some reason, some excuse, some explanation. For this there was none. Looking back, I cannot even blame the aphrodisiac ointment; I knew its action, I had had experience of how I reacted to it, I need not have joined Tibby there. And yet, of my own free will, when she pulled me down at her side, I did not draw away but threw my arms around her, drew her close, and felt, with a mingling of surprise and tenderness, the rise of desire as her soft lips parted under mine.

For everything else so far that strange summer I had known some precedent, some experience. Here I was wholly ignorant, still startled—although intellectually I knew it could happen to anyone—that I was physically responding to another woman's touch.

Tibby's hands, narrow and fine, lingered half-painfully, half-excitingly on my breasts. We lay there lazily caressing each other, each feeling the other's breasts hardening under our hands, the nipples rising and softening and rising again. She seemed to sense my mixture of hunger and inexperience, to realize that I was not quite certain how to proceed, and taking the initiative, pushed me back against the bolsters. She parted my knees with a nudge of her own. Then, as we lay pressed together, breasts touching, lips lightly seeking in repeated, playful kisses, her seeking hands found the center of passion, and with clever touches, first lightly, then more and more intensely, she excited me until I began, first to move in response to her touch and to moan, then until I was throbbing wildly, at the very edge of climax. Then, laughing, she let her caresses quiet and die away, waiting until my breathing quieted, then beginning again.

But this time I was no passive participant; my own hands sought for the softness between her legs and with a curious shock of strangeness and familiarity, found the hot dampness there; I felt that curious duality, myself and another, familiar emotions and strange ones, as my fingers moved on the soft contours and touched the small, hot, throbbing center. It was strangely exciting to hear her gasp of response, and I began trying to elicit it again, to tease and play with her and create greater and greater response. It was as if each twitching nerve in Tibby was hooked up to a similar thread of response in me;

her growing excitement roused me to wild response, and we clutched one another, gasping wildly, again and again coming to the wild edge of climax and letting ourselves slide back. A random glance across the room showed me a blurred image in the mirror, soft curves, long loose hair streaking our faces, Tibby's great eyes widening and dilating with excited pleasure. Then it spun out of focus again and I heard her moan with excitement. "No more playing—now—oh, now, now, I want it—" and then her seagull cry of pleasure and the frenzied grip of her thighs on my hand. "No, no, no more—no more—"

And then something exploded inside me, so wildly that I thought I would faint, the inward clutch of wild tension and the mad flooding release.

Tibby shook her hair out of her eyes. She sat up, smiled at me and said, "Wow!"

I laughed, a singular mixture of embarrassment and warmth. Tibby laughed too, and said, "I told you: it could be fun. It's a good way to spend a boring summer afternoon. Nobody could be bored with you around, I imagine."

There was a curious intimacy about us as we dressed. I helped her button the back of her blouse; she came and stroked my hair as I sat at the dressing table combing my red locks into place.

She said at last, gently, "Sara, I have to say one thing. I want to be your friend—I *am* your friend. But I can't stand up for you against Matthew. I won't, and you mustn't ask it of me. Short of that—well, you are new to this, and I don't want to see you hurt. If your witch-memory returns in time, you won't be, but if it doesn't—"

I interrupted, "Tibby, do one thing for me. Without playing any games at all—do you believe that this thing exists? This stuff about being the soul of an immortal witch?"

"I must believe it," she said. "I've *seen* it. It came back for a moment downstairs—didn't it, Sara? If it returns again, you'll be all right—even though I may have to fight you, just as I'd have fought Sara herself—the older Sara. But you can fight, then, on even terms.

What's worrying me now is what will happen if it doesn't return. At
the Esbat—have you any idea of what will happen, what will be expected of you?"

"No, but it doesn't matter. I've decided that I'm not going."

"And how do you intend to stay away if Matthew Hay wants you
there? Answer me that!"

"Easy," I said, "I just won't go. I won't interfere, it's nothing to
me what other people do, but I want no part of it. I shall stay home
and read a good book."

Her laughter sounded despairing. "In that case I can only wish
you a lot of luck! You'll need it. Do you think no one has tried to
avoid the Esbats or Sabbats? No, Sara. You'll be there. And if your
memory hasn't returned—listen, I ought to prepare you—"

"I don't want to hear," I said. "Please go now, Tibby." I leaned
over and kissed her. "Yes, I'm still your friend, but without all this
witch-nonsense. Let's just forget all that."

She sat hesitant for some time, then drew on her leather moc-
casins and got up to go. She said slowly, "On your own head, then.
Remember I tried," and went out the door and down the stairs.

NINE

THE COVEN GATHERS

AFTER THE HECTIC TENSION OF THE FIRST COUPLE OF DAYS, THE pace slowed until I began actually to wonder if everything that had happened to me, in that first chaotic forty-eight hours in the Latimer house, had been the result of nervous shock combined with an overactive imagination. That evening, Brian came to take me out to dinner and I dressed in my best and most fashionable New York clothes, intending to knock his eye out and to hell with the local farmers. As we passed the next farm on our way to Arkham, I saw Tibby carrying a milk-pail toward the barn and waved to her with a sudden flood of sympathy. Poor kid, maybe I could encourage her to get away before I left; to Boston, Providence, New York. This was no life for anyone. Tied to an ignorant family and a brutal routine of farm work and housekeeping, no wonder she found her only excitement in morbid evocation of the old witch-cult.

Brian saw the gesture. "You know Tibby?"

"She dropped in this afternoon to welcome me—a neighborly gesture." I managed not to blush.

"Well, she's a bit of a protégée of the old lady's; I guess Whit-fields and Latimers have been close for centuries, she's probably some sort of distant relation. I must confess I don't care much for her—she makes it all too obvious that she'd welcome some excitement from the new young doctor. But I'm not the kind of man who could follow in Matthew Hay's footsteps."

Which, of course, put an end before I ever really considered it, to any thoughts of confessing everything to him and asking for advice on how to handle the fixed local notion that I was Aunt Sara reborn.

I enjoyed Brian's company as much as ever, and went gladly back to the house he shared with his cousin to spend a few hours at the beginning of the night. This could, I now realized, grow to be something very real and very good. If only I could be free of the pervasive fear that I would suffer a repetition of the curious possession which had forced me to behave in strange ways, ask strange and unexpected questions, lash out against people I did not really know . . .

I was painting again the next morning, the first of the set of illustrations racing toward conclusion, when the peal of the doorbell summoned me downstairs. Matthew Hay, lean, saturnine and compelling, stood on the doorstep.

"I just dropped by to remind you that this is the night of the full moon," he said, "and we meet two hours after sunset, outside the Church of the Antique Rite. Since you are new, and your memories have not fully returned, you need not bring anything—you've done your share of providing food and wine and materials in the past."

My stomach gave an unpleasant little lurch. He took all this so completely for granted. But somehow I must manage to stand up against him.

I said, "I'm sorry, Matthew. But after thinking it over, I've decided—" what was Tibby's phrase?—"this isn't the kind of game I want to play. Witchcraft and covens have no appeal for me. I appreciate your kindness in wanting to welcome me back, if you believe that's what you're doing. But I'm not my Aunt Sara, Matthew, and I'm not interested in the things she was interested in. So let's, please, drop the subject?"

I had never believed that "he turned black with rage" was anything but a cliché used by bad writers of pulp fiction, but now I saw it in action. His face grew so dark and congested with fury that his skin seemed three shades darker.

He said, "What the hell—!"

"No hell at all. I don't believe in hell. And incidentally I don't believe in devils, demons, witches or any of the rest of it. I'm sorry, but my mind is made up. And now, if you don't mind, I'm working; I have a book to finish. Please excuse me."

I turned to go inside. He reached out with the swiftness of a snake striking, and gripped my wrist.

He said, "If Tibby's put you up to this, if she's threatened you or played jealous, I'll break her neck!"

"On the contrary." I tried to jerk my wrist away. "Tibby couldn't have been nicer, and she was very, very persuasive. No, it's entirely my own decision, Matt, so don't blame her. Let go of me!" I wrenched away, with a spasm of rage. "Look, how *dare* you come here like this?"

"You know how I dare," he said slowly, "and you can't deny it."

I chose willfully to misunderstand. "If you think that because I let you have sex with me, you can order me around the way you do that poor harmless kid Tibby, you get another think, right away!"

"That isn't what I mean. It's what you *are,* Sara. Damn it, I thought I had you convinced, and just a little time away from us, you begin doubting again, and refusing to believe in your own powers!"

"Oh, powers be *damned,*" I yelled at him. I found myself wishing, for once, that I had the strength of Aunt Sara, to turn on him and blast hell out of his stupid arrogance. When I'd turned momentarily on Tibby, speaking to her in what must have been Aunt Sara's voice, she had turned pale with fright. I wished I could think of some way to scare Matthew Hay like that. I drew a deep breath—

The room wavered before me, I felt myself seeming to swell up, ready to strike with fury. *How dared he—this man who owed me all of his power—*

I took one step toward him. I saw him step backward, startled—and then I saw the quick, concealed smirk on his face.

Had he been trying to evoke this response?

It was one thing to summon up Aunt Sara in a rage—and another to get rid of her again! I clenched my fists, fighting against the black torrent of alien thoughts and memories, the blasting power and strength inside me that was like a remorseless tidal wave . . .

Then it was gone, and I unclenched my fists. I said in the quietest, most common-sense voice I could manage, "I believe I may have had some—delusions here. The house is getting on my nerves. I think any reputable psychologist would advise me to keep clear of anything which might stimulate further experiences of this kind. And even coming to your—what is it?"

"Esbat—"

"Even coming as an onlooker or guest might have that effect on me. So thank you very much, but—no, thank you. Now, excuse me; I really must work." I went into the house and shut the door, quickly bolting it on the inside. I heard him try the door, but when he realized it was locked he went away again, and after a while, looking through the leaded-glass panes by the front door, I saw him going across the fields toward the Whitfield farm. Upstairs I tried to resume my interrupted painting, but the mood had been destroyed, and I quickly realized that if I persisted I would spoil everything I had done. I longed for Brian, and wished there was a telephone in the house; I was far too isolated here.

The house seemed to echo emptily around me. I fixed myself a sandwich for lunch, but found I could hardly swallow it. Why was I so unnerved? I had, after all, stood up clearly enough to Matthew Hay in an open altercation. I'd won that round. It was only later that I began to identify the cause of my unease. He had been bested too easily; he would hardly give up at this, and next time it might be the iron fist without even the velvet glove.

I felt I could not bear to stay in the house waiting for his next move, whatever it might be. Then it occurred to me; the Arkham-Innsmouth bus went by the corner at eleven-twenty this morning, and it was barely eleven now. I could go and spend the day in Arkham, perhaps explore the campus of the University, check on art supplies in the college bookstore—I needed a small sable brush anyhow—go to a movie, perhaps, for Arkham, a town of nineteen thousand, must have at least one cinema house—and perhaps even go to a hotel for the night. If I wasn't here, they couldn't do anything to get me to their old Esbat.

Swiftly I packed a couple of things into a big handbag which had served me before this as a weekend case, dressed in city clothes—a cool green pantsuit—changed my flat sneakers for city sandals with medium heels, and set out down the road for the bus stop. The road led past the Whitfield farm, but I had no fear of encountering Matthew on the road; I already knew that he preferred to cut across the fields.

It was high summer, and the canes of the blackberries were laden; I walked along briskly, stopping now and then to pick a ripe berry which hung over the road, and put it into my mouth. They were delicious, with a flavor city-grown frozen berries never attained. My spirits lifted with every step I took away from the Latimer house. Perhaps I could leave a message for Brian, or telephone him, from Arkham, at the hospital. If he was on duty at the hospital we might have a bite together when he was free.

A light, familiar voice called, "Sara!"

My elated mood collapsed. Nevertheless I kept up my pace. Tibby came across the field to the road, looking twelve years old in faded, grubby blue jeans and a man's shirt with the sleeves cut away, far too tight for her.

"Hullo, Tibby. But I can't talk now, I have a bus to catch. I'm going to Arkham for the day, and I may not be back tonight."

Her eyes glittered briefly. She said, "You can't do that. You know you can't. It's full moon. Have you forgotten what tonight is?"

I gave an impatient sigh. I didn't want to discuss this all over again. I said, "No, I haven't. That's why I'm going. Look, Tibby, Matthew must have told you this, I saw him come toward your place. You've got him all to yourself, and I wish you joy of him. Tib, be a pal, get out of my way and let me catch my bus."

She said, quietly, "You know you aren't going, Sara."

"Tibby, I don't want to be nasty, but do you really think you can *stop* me?"

"I'd rather not," she said surprisingly. "If it were up to me, I would let you go, and good riddance. But Matthew wants you to stay, and what Matthew wants, he shall have as long as it's up to me."

Her next move startled me; she jerked her head around and gave a long shrill whistle. I wondered for a moment if she was summoning reinforcements, but nothing happened except a small flutter in the hedges, and a black bird flew down, hopped briefly in the road before us, then flapped up to Tibby's shoulder and sat there, croaking hoarsely, "Good girl! Good girl!"

"What in the world is that, Tibby?"

"A jackdaw," she said briefly, "I taught him to speak myself. You should know, you have Ginger Tom—no, you call him Barnabas now, don't you? Look, Sara, don't make me do this. There's no point to it. You know you have to do what Matthew wants, just as I do, until you are powerful enough to defy him, and you're not that powerful now. *Don't* make me, Sara. Please. I like you."

"I liked you, too," I said dryly, "but you're putting a hell of a strain on our friendship."

The bird croaked, "Go back! Go back!" With a long shrill whistle, he added, "Full moon! Full moon! Whee! Good girl!"

"I'll admire your pet some other time, Tibby. I don't want to miss the bus." I began to walk past her. Finding her directly in my way, I started to walk round.

She turned her head and crooned softly to the jackdaw. Though she spoke clearly, I could not understand a word, as if she spoke some foreign language. I decided not to waste any more time talking, and began to walk past.

I have no explanation for what happened next. The evil eyes of the bird seemed to hold mine, and as I began to walk past, I discovered that once again, I was walking directly toward Tibby, that she was directly in my path. I swerved to walk around her, and whether she moved, or I changed direction without knowing it, there she was right before me again. Once again I altered my direction; yet again I found Tibby and the evil bird right in my way, so that I could not continue without walking right through her.

Her blue eyes rested on mine, almost compassionately, and she said, "I told you I couldn't let you go, Sara. Try another direction."

"I'm catching that bus."

"You're not, you know," she said.

We must have maneuvered together in the road for a considerable time. She did not touch me. She only stayed where she was, and try as I might to pass her, I found my feet repeatedly bearing me directly into her path. Finally I heard the roar of an aging, wheezing motor; over the brow of the hill, it roared past in a cloud of dust. Tibby whistled and the jackdaw flew up, wheeled briefly and flew into the hedge. I found that I could walk freely again.

"Go where you please now," she said indifferently, "the bus is gone, and there's no other way to get out of town."

"I won't forget this, Tibby."

"I hope you won't," she said. "Oh, Sara, why bother being angry?

You know why I had to do it. I warned you I couldn't stand up to Matthew for you."

I had nothing further to say; I turned and began to walk back toward my house. I could have burst into frantic, terrified tears. There was an odd reason I didn't; I knew Tibby would come and try to comfort me, and that she would be perfectly sincere. I couldn't have borne it.

I went back to my house, and sat without moving in the cold kitchen. I felt rather like a rat in a trap. I had congratulated myself on coming off victor against Matthew in the first round, but Tibby had beaten me handily in this one, without even trying. I wasn't sure what their next move would be—they could hardly come in, if I locked all my doors, and drag me off bodily to the Esbat; and even if they did, I'd bet that I could disrupt the proceedings, even if I only stood up and started singing "Onward Christian Soldiers" at the top of my voice.

Barnabas mewed disconsolately at the kitchen door. I was in no mood to worry about cats, but I let him in and opened a can of cat food. "Where the hell were you this morning when I needed you," I demanded, with the blackest of humor. "Why didn't you come and catch that blasted jackdaw and rip it to bits!"

He sidled past me and began gobbling down his food, and I told myself I was getting as crazy as the rest of them. Damn it, I needed someone sane like Brian!

Maybe if he was going to Arkham this afternoon, to the hospital, he could take me with him. Maybe at least I could arrange to spend the night with him, not here overlooking the graveyard where Matthew and his stupid coven would be cavorting around at their rituals, which were sure to be either idiotic or obscene, or more probably both.

I let Barnabas finish his meal, put him outside—there was no telling when I'd be back—and fetching my big handbag, set off again, this time to walk to Madison Corners. It was a little over a mile, but I wasn't worrying about that. I confess I walked uneasily as I passed the Whitfield farm, but there was no sign of life there; only a big black bird flapped in the hedge as I passed, and to me one big black bird looks just like any other, so I had no idea whether it was the one Tibby called her familiar.

My spirits slowly lifted as I came within sight of the little cross-roads town. Soon I would be talking to Brian or perhaps seeing Colin. The corner store had a telephone; I found Brian's number in the Arkham phone book (Standish Brian MD, Mad Corn) and dialed it; after it rang four times, a strange voice came on and identified itself as the answering service. "I'm very sorry, the doctor has gone out on a call toward Innsmouth. He sent a message that he may not be back until very late tonight. Would you like me to have Doctor James Standish call you?"

I thanked the anonymous voice and hung up, dejection sinking deep in me. Brian would not be back until late tonight—by which time Matthew Hay might have moved again to get me to his Esbat. I bought myself an ice-cream pop from the freezer box in the store and lingered, looking at a display of chicken feed, not wanting to go back to the house, alone.

"You figuring on getting yourself some chickens, Miss Sara?" said a voice behind me. "I can let you have a few hens and a rooster nice and cheap."

I turned to face a strange farmer. He said, "Sorry to be casual, Miss; reckon everybody round these parts knows who you are. I'm Raboth Tate; I raise chickens for the market, and like I say, if you want a few I can make you a good price on 'em."

"I haven't decided," I said. "I'm not even sure I'll be here more than a week or so."

"I can let you have chickens for the pot too, less'n you get them from Nahum Whitfield; I saw you've took up friendly with his daughter."

"That's kind of you, Mr. Tate; I haven't made any arrangements about chickens with Mr. Whitfield, although I had intended to ask Tibby about eggs and milk. A chicken fricassee would taste good." I would fix it, with Mother's hot biscuits, for Brian tomorrow night or whenever he was free. "But for just now, I wonder if you know anyone around here who's driving toward Arkham this afternoon? I missed the bus this morning, and I need a few things I can't get here, paintbrushes and such."

"Paintbrushes over here," he said, nodding at a display of house paint, gallon buckets of whitewash and brushes six inches wide. I laughed and said, "Not that kind; I mean for oil paints."

"Oh, you mean *artist's* brushes! Yes, I reckon you'd have to go in town for those."

"Is anyone local going? I'd be happy to pay for the ride."

"No call for that," Raboth Tate said. "Neighbors here always be glad to give you a ride, only I don't expect anyone be going tonight—figuring on what day it is. Ain't *nobody* going out of town tonight." He paused and said with curious emphasis, "I reckoned Matt Hay had done told you about that."

Oh, God, he was one of them too! I don't remember to this day how I got out of the store, or anything else very clearly, until I found myself stumbling blindly along Witch Hill Road, almost at my own door again.

I sat in a numb daze for almost an hour, trying desperately to think of what to do. All that came to my mind was that I should go upstairs, bolt the door, not answer the doorbell, and let them do their damnedest. They couldn't exactly drag me there, could they? After that exhibition this morning with Tibby and the jackdaw, I wasn't so sure that they couldn't get me there somehow, with my will or without it, but they'd have to get to me first.

I wondered if I was getting paranoid. There must be more harmless farmers than witches and warlocks around. Was I getting delusions of persecution? Vaguely I remembered that during the height of the "button" craze, a friend of mine had worn one that read "Even paranoids have real enemies." I felt like that now, shut up in Aunt Sara's house, not daring to put my nose outside for fear Matthew Hay, or Tibby, would come by and get the best of me again. And the worst, most fearsome enemy was inside myself; the memory of the times I had found myself behaving like Aunt Sara!

The afternoon wore on. I tried to bestir myself in the house, but everything I took up made me wonder when Aunt Sara had last touched it, and I finally gave it up again, and took up a paperback detective story I'd brought with me from New York, trying to lose myself in the exploits of a red-headed detective with two girl friends and two clients, and a fresh bottle of whiskey for each.

Maybe I should have fortified myself with a drink, but I had a deadly fear of losing full consciousness if Matthew Hay tried any other argument or trick. I needed all my wits about me.

It seemed ages until sunset. I began listlessly cooking myself some supper—potatoes in the oven, more eggs, the typical spinster supper. I was slicing tomatoes for a salad when a timid rap came at the back door.

I ignored it, but when it came again, went to look out. It didn't sound like Matthew's firm knuckled stroke. And I couldn't imagine Tibby being that timid.

Outside on the doorstep, a tall, slender woman stood, carrying a basket.

I told myself not to be completely paranoid. This woman was obviously a harmless neighbor. I turned off the fire under my eggs and opened the door.

She blinked. She was somewhere in her fifties, a slim, healthy-looking woman with apple cheeks, in a print housedress.

"My word," she said, "Matt did tell me about the likeness, but I never believed how strong it could be! I was a friend of your Aunt Sara, dear; I'm Judith Hay. Matt sent me along to apologize for sounding so dictatorial this afternoon, he said you have to do what you want—does that make sense to you, dear?"

It did; I nodded.

Brian had mentioned her to me; but she looked harmless enough. "My brother tends to forget everybody's not the fanatic that he is," she said. "I brought you some of my strawberry shortcake, dear; I thought it would go good with your supper. Here, take the basket, and if I were you I'd set it in a cool place. No, I won't come in now, Sara; some other time. I hope you like the strawberries, dear, I picked them myself fresh this morning. Goodbye," and she thrust the basket at me and whisked away.

I took the basket inside, taking away the clean white napkin which covered the top. The strawberries were enticingly red and juicy, the biscuit crust brown and nutty and delicious looking. I lifted out the plate, thinking that I wished I dared eat it. It might have been drugged. Were they that subtle? Could I take the chance?

The bottom of the plate appeared to be covered with something thin and sticky; I rubbed my hands together to get it off, and succeeded only in smearing it all over the palms. I raised my hands to my face and sniffed. It was a sharp, herbal smell, curiously dark and excremental; I rubbed my hands together, feeling an unpleasant sick dizziness.

The unguent works quickly . . .

I dropped the basket on the floor, hearing somewhere in the periphery of fading consciousness that the plate fell and crashed. *Too bad.* Darkness wavered, closed around my eyes. *I've been poisoned, drugged.* I staggered to the sofa in the living room and lowered myself at the last instant before I fell, aware in a last blinding moment of clarity that I had forgotten to bolt the door.

Only it no longer seemed to matter.

TEN

ORGY AT MOONRISE

I HAVE NEVER KNOWN HOW LONG I LAY THERE IN A DARK DREAM, strange dark swirls coming and going in my mind, like great waves of darkness breaking over me, washing up, receding, then breaking again. Pointless phrases kept repeating and reverberating over and over in my head, echoing as if my mind were an empty corridor and someone was shouting down it, raising echoes:

"Horse, hattock, to horse and away!"

"Af baraldim Azathoth!"

"Aklo, aklo, dors de ma main . . ."

And a painfully endless sequence in which I was squatting motionless in a dark expanse of nowhere, with a voice endlessly repeating; "What are you doing?" "I'm minding my mavin." "What are you doing?" "Minding my mavin," again and again, with an idiot seriousness, as if the words reiterated a meaningful and important responsibility. (To this day I have not lost hope that somewhere in the dark corners of my subconscious, a meaning will emerge for the words.) And all through this, waves of sickness came and went, as if my aching, retching body were chained down somewhere, struggling in the darkness, while the real me flapped and muttered somewhere in a realm filled with greyish light and strange iridescent sparkles behind my eyes. *An overdose can give you one hell of a bad trip.* Once, in Berkeley, in the innocent days when acid was regarded as no more serious than illegal drinking, back before it became the policeman's paranoid equivalent to the Moors murder or the Manson case, I had tripped out on acid, and once I had been stuck in an apparently timeless series of words reverberating in my head, which had worn off harmlessly with no side effects except a lasting dislike for certain kinds of rock lyrics which kept repeating; but under acid I had never had this overpowering, deathly sickness, this sense of—how can I put it?—as if the hallucinations were reality, and the retching, muttering body down there somewhere were the illusion.

After a period of time about which I knew nothing except that it must have seemed longer than it was—after all, I could hardly have lain there hallucinating for three or four days, which is what it felt like—I heard the door open softly. There were footsteps in the hall. A small secret spot in me still cried out with rebellion and fear; the rest of my self *knew,* and welcomed.

"Sara?"

"Don't be a fool. She's way out where words don't mean a damn thing."

That's what you think. But I hugged to myself the awareness that I heard. It would be my secret. I heard myself giggle secretly. With my eyes shut I could see the dark forms coming into the room.

"Moonrise."

The moonlight was inside my eyelids, so that I walked with closed eyes in a curious colorless light and the forms bending over me had weird shapes, forms to match the jagged quality of their voices.

"Handle her with reverence. The Horned One will be angry if she is hurt."

Mocking laughter somewhere. I could see the Horned One, in the double mask that was half laughter and half deep grief.

Someone said to me gently, "It is time to go." I knew that gentle voice, reached out for the soft curves of it. Bodiless hands raised my body, and with the touch I felt myself flying upward through the colorless astral light.

"How shall we travel?"

"Fly, fly! The broomsticks await!"

The room vanished. Someone thrust a broomstick between my hands. Of course. How else would a witch fly to the Black Sabbath? I climbed astride it. It felt soft, like a great phallic organ, between my hands, too enormous for entering, but nevertheless come to welcome and comfort me. I stroked it lovingly. In a tiny fragment of awareness I was half conscious of movement, of steps, of painfully putting one step before the other, hands guiding me. I was dreaming, of course, the hands and the movement had to be a dream.

"Ride out! Ride out! Sisters and brothers of the Dark One, take to the sky!"

The air was cold on my face; the motion of the broomstick between my legs was for a moment a ridiculous hopping, then it leaped upward and I saw the stars spring back as I flew straight into the great, red, exploding moon. Around me the sky was full of witches, dark shapes on broomsticks, hunched, great, Barnabas perched on one of them, Tibby's jackdaw with human eyes, his great dark wings expanded to condor size as he kept stroke with my flight. The moon was enormous but I saw the light only through my closed eyelids, and through closed eyes, too, the village and houses spread out below me, the horizon vast, stretching to the weird gabled roofs of Arkham far below me. The landscape was oddly colored and angled, like a photographic negative. I felt the thunder of demons moving inside the earth and retched at their sickening smell as the ground heaved; the stones in the old graveyard moved and trembled and white things came crawling, wormlike, from under them.

I opened my eyes to a blaze of candlelight. The ruined church opened out around me, the real church, only the Earth-version of the real, the demonic church spreading vastly out beyond, with the blasted oak and the gallows where I had once been hanged, dogs snarling from the pit beyond where they had once licked my blood.

Through the candlelight the Horned God came walking. I had gone too far even to hear the cries and the chants, but I saw him clearly, a huge naked male figure, at least nine feet tall, although the size wavered and varied like a shadow by the light of a flickering candle. Now he seemed small enough that I could pick him up in the palm of my hand and gobble him down like a barley-sugar man: now his figure swooped and soared up to such a vast height that he touched the rooftree. His penis was huge, long, dyed red at the tip. He wore nothing but a necklet on which was strung a silver five-pointed star, and the monstrous horned mask.

His voice reverberated, a voice I knew and yet did not know, Matthew Hay's voice but made huge and echoing as if he was shouting through a speaking-trumpet.

"Welcome, welcome to our priestess! We greet you after seven years in the bonds of death!"

His hand moved to the ash of the ritual fire, smearing my breasts with a strange design. The shout wavered up from the dark forms beyond, where I saw them, men and women, young and old, dark and pale, mother-naked, distorted into witch-forms in the wandering sickly light. I floated away again and when I came up to consciousness I saw them, couple by couple, approaching the fire and backing away leaping, flying, shouting. The curious, sickening smell was all over and through me. And beyond them and their formless bodies I saw skeletons, walking death, legions of the dead, and still beyond those, thronging fairy forms, bright and strange. Their faces glowing with light—of course, I thought, that's the light that never was on sea or land. The witches capered and shouted and the great form of the Horned God held me, stretched out suspended in midair over the altar. His great erect organ thrust out before him and in suspension of awareness, I clutched at it. The sickness had worn off now, although the greyish astral light was still around me and I still saw better with my eyes closed. The smell of death and of herbs was in my nostrils, and the Horned God was floating over me, bodiless.

He touched my naked breasts with one demanding finger and I felt them leaping up to stand at attention and salute his huge penis. My eyes were closed, but I saw far more clearly than I had ever done in the bright sunlight. My skin was alive, covered with a million tiny hungry mouths, each one aching to be kissed, filled.

"Azathoth! Hertha! Cernunnus! Astarte! Ishtar!" the Horned God cried. "Witness! Witness the return of the priestess and consecrate her here, upon this altar!"

He leaped at me—to my strained and extended consciousness it seemed that he made a great leap through space, floating high in the air—his weight came down on me and he drove relentlessly into my body. At first I felt only pain and a wild sense of shock that brought me for a single moment up into reality, aware that this was no dream, that some of it, at least, was true, then the world spun out again and I lay on an immense, prehistoric monolith, my body painted with strange, glowing signs, while above me the monstrous, inhuman Horned God hovered, driving into me again and again until I heard myself scream, partly with pain and partly with wild excitement. All around me, the wild howling and strange chants went on, and I saw face after face swim out of the luminous darkness. At the edge of the circle, by the haunted firelight, they dropped two by two, or in threes, coupling there in a maddened animal frenzy, and I saw it all at the fringes of vision while I lay there, my body gripped in the hard animal's paws of the Horned One. An old woman, face lined and withered but with the smooth loins and flat belly of a young woman, lay writhing in the arms of a hairy, thick-shouldered youth with eyes as small as a pig's; a fairylike delicate young girl lay gasping, her mouth open with screams of pleasure, below the brutish form of old Jeb from the store. A thin sensuous woman, naked and familiar, with glowing cat's eyes, crouched below the monstrous body of what seemed a misshapen beast—or was it a man in a mask?—who drove into her from behind, his great hips moving remorselessly, his organ like a mighty piston, rising and falling. And like the driving of machinery, too, was the immense thing hovering over me, driving, working, gasping in repeated, endless rhythm. It went on and on. On and on. The night had paled, it seemed that days and days of cloudless skies had come and gone while I lay beneath the Horned One, my body vibrating, exploding, before finally, with a great cry, he thrashed about, clawing at my breasts, and fell motionless above me.

"The Sacred Marriage has been consummated! Hear and witness, ye Dark Ones of the Woods!"

Is it over? I wondered. But it was not. The fire blazed up toward the rooftop, so that I wondered if outside the woods were on fire. Someone held a cup of wine to my lips. It tasted sharp and real. Tibby murmured, "Sara, are you all right?"

Someone muttered behind me, "The unguent should be losing its effect about now, and she should be coming out of it."

"Not if she got the kind of overdose we had to put on the plate to make sure she got *enough.*"

The words spun out into meaningless gibberish, and I heard myself crying out words that made no sense. I heard the shrill cries of a jackdaw, syllables like nonsense, echoing and reverberating. A strange form bent over me where I lay still motionless. He leaned over, gripped me briefly and entered me, penetrating deeply and roughly. I gasped and cried out, but someone behind me was holding my hands. It was very fast and all over in a few seconds; he reeled away from me, and another dark form took his place.

It seemed that this was repeated endlessly in the next few days or hours—or minutes?—a heavy male form would loom above me, all eyes and huge erection; then would come the harsh thrust, without tenderness, between my legs, the rough mindless movement, the explosion of passion, and the unknown would vanish in the darkness. At first I lay in a dark daze of horror, swaying in mindless terror and pain, but then, against my will, what was happening down there in the darkness began to reach me, to rouse me, and I began to respond, moving with the great thrust inward, gasping, writhing, crying out with a great shriek of passion as the lust of the witch expended itself inward. I have no idea how often this cycle was repeated, but I know it was many times. And finally it repeated itself again and again only in dreams, for the dark forms were gone, slipping away into darkness, and I spun outward and back, rocking like a vast pendulum, turning and spinning with the very motion of the earth. And at last there was nothing but darkness and silence, whirling, and the murmuring of the trees.

I stirred and woke. *God, what a nightmare!* I'd heard that the frenzied orgies of the Witches' Sabbat were due to delirium from the strange hallucinatory drugs they used, and somebody had evidently slipped me some. Had I lain here in the sofa all night, wildly hallucinating orgies and nightmares and gang-rape at a witches' coven? What a freak-out! My subconscious was evidently filled up with this filthy crud!

I felt sick and dizzy, with a torturing thirst. I blinked, sitting up, then gazed around wildly, in dawning terror. I was no longer on the sofa in the old living room. I was no longer wearing my sweater and jeans.

I was lying in the old graveyard, all alone, stark naked, with the thin grey rain of dawn falling softly on my face.

ELEVEN

THE MORNING AFTER THE NIGHT BEFORE

I FELT MY MIND BREAKING LOOSE FROM ITS MOORINGS, AND fought, with a breathless sense of unreality, to hang on to sanity.

Had it all happened, then?

Had I really been taken to a Witches' Sabbat—no, Esbat—where I was ritually raped on a strange altar by a Horned God, then gang-raped by the assembled—could I call them worshipers? (What a word! Assembled blasphemers would be better!) Congregation, anyway.

No. Some part of it, at least, must have been a dream, or nightmare, or hallucination. The flying through space, the Horned God, the immense circling monoliths. But the rest of it?

I still felt sick and dazed. I got up, wincing at the touch of sharp grass, pebbles and sticks under my bare feet. I was in sight of the road, but no one ever came up this road, especially at this hour of a Sunday morning. Shivering in the icy rain, which was growing heavier by the moment—had it been the rain that weakened me?—I decided that at least I had better get inside, out of it, though I was wet already; at least my hair was wet and getting wetter—I made my way shakily into the house. The kitchen was as I remembered it last night, although someone—had I done it in the last minute before passing out?—had turned off the oven, and turned off the fire under the eggs. My salad lay wilted in the bowl, a half-peeled tomato and a knife still on the cutting board beside them.

I remembered the basket, and Judith Hay's strawberry shortcake, and the drugged paste on the plate. *Of course;* they couldn't be sure I'd eat the stuff, maybe I was allergic to strawberries or just didn't like them, but they knew that I'd have to handle the plate.

But there was no sign of plate, basket or strawberries.

So they took it away again.

Sara, don't be paranoid.

I was still icy cold, my body racked by shudders of cold and terror. I went upstairs and ran the hottest bath I could stand, and crawled into it, lying neck-deep in the warm water until the shiver quieted down.

Had any of it really happened?

Had I simply had the world's worst nightmare?

Had I been drugged, and been on the lousiest of all bad trips?

Had I walked in my sleep, or my delirium, out into the old graveyard?

Had Matthew Hay and his witch-coven, angry at my refusal to take Aunt Sara's place, simply carried me out there while I was unconscious, as an act of filthy revenge, or as a perverted, sick practical joke? Any man who seriously believed in witchcraft in this day and age—Satanism, that is, not the harmless earth religion sometimes called by that name, only didn't they call it Wicca? Anyhow, not Wicca, but whatever it was Matthew Hay thought he was doing, that medieval mess of witch-hunting, devil-calling—or whatever it was—or demon-worship would have to be pretty sick inside.

Or—and this started up the shuddering again, even in the near-boiling bath—had it all been true, simply blown up and made fantastical by my drugged state? I had certainly walked, or been carried, instead of—as I clearly remembered—flying there on a broomstick. One fire or maybe two might have been multiplied to a vast ring of them. The Horned God might well have been Matthew Hay in a mask, and it had seemed so real simply because my reality-testing was at low ebb. As for the rape, well, there was nothing supernatural about that. *It wouldn't have been the first time, anyway.*

And the multiple rapes afterward, thousands and thousands of them, it had seemed? Well, that could have been delirium, and a few local louts or farmers; pretty sick, but hardly what it had seemed. Half a dozen such episodes (and had it really been rape? I hadn't resisted!) could have been multiplied, in my freaked-out state, to seem like a great many.

Use your head, Sara. Think.

Don't panic.

How much of the rape had been real?

Climbing out of the tub, I examined my naked body. I felt terribly stiff and sore, and there were many bruises, even scratches, but I could not tell whether these were left over from the first episode with Matthew, or whether some of them might be fresh. In any case, some of the scratches could be from briars and brambles in the garden and graveyard.

My mind still felt fuzzy. I put on my warmest bathrobe, went downstairs, and made myself a cup of extra-strong tea, and laced it more liberally than usual with sugar; I needed the strength.

Sipping it, and feeling warmth return to my aching bones, I realized that, even though I felt better, the hot bath had been a mistake. It could have washed away any remaining proofs. I should have come back here, grabbed a few clothes, run all the way to Madison Corners if necessary, and gotten on the phone to the State Police.

Would they have believed a word I said?

Yes, if my body had still been bearing traces of an orgy—semen, bloodstains, even the smoke of the fires or the remnants of the drugged unguent. But now? I had seen how the liberal California police treated hippies coming down from acid trips. How would the backwoods police out here treat a solitary woman who told a wild tale of having been drugged, raped, and dumped naked in a graveyard? Would they even bother to make tests? Especially when it was all mixed up with wild tales of witches' covens? And Matthew Hay could have come forward and testified that I had fallen quite willingly into sex with him.

Barnabas slithered in through the kitchen door. His yellow fur was damp with rain. "You certainly were a lot of help last night," I said to him. But what did I expect? He was a cat—a witch's cat—not a watchdog.

He jumped on the kitchen table, nosing at my cup of tea. I gave him a piece of buttered bread; he nosed it disdainfully, but finally decided it was edible. That suited me fine. I hadn't the energy to open cans right now. The kitchen clock told me it was half-past six.

I tried desperately to think of what to do next. I could pack and run, abandon the house (or sell it to Matthew Hay, that was what he wanted all along anyhow) and go back to New York.

But would they let me go? Tibby had somehow managed to stop me yesterday, when I had only wanted to get on a bus.

I was still feeling miserably sick and dizzy, probably the after-effects of whatever drugs had been in that damned unguent. *If you get an overdose you can have a hell of a bad trip.* Well, I'd had one, a trip straight to hell. *If you get too much of an overdose you can be poisoned.* I had certainly been poisoned; my vision was still blurred, my head throbbed as if I'd been beaten, and my whole body ached, down to the bones; I felt almost frantically hungry but even the sweetened tea made my stomach churn and I was afraid to eat anything else for fear it would all come up again.

Even as I sat at the table, it all seemed to sway and swell up around me, and I had for a moment to hold on to the chair for fear I'd fall off.

It was too early to do anything, even to go to the State Police. If I rushed off half-cocked, with the drugs still in my system, blurring my judgment, I might find myself en route to the funny farm, more properly the State Hospital, and even though I could probably prove my sanity sooner or later, I would probably have a long and unpleasant interlude before getting loose. At the very least it would play hob with any chances of finishing my book illustration assignment.

I moved shakily around, making sure all the doors were bolted, even that small effort taxing my small reserves of strength. Talk about locking the stable door after the horse, et cetera! Oooh, I was sick!

What I needed now was *rest*. I staggered upstairs and fell into Aunt Sara's bed, dragging the quilt up over my head. Barnabas perched inquisitively on the bedpost, then jumped down, nudging up to me, kneading me with comforting paws, purring like a lullaby, finally nestling down at my side. Secure in the knowledge of the bolted doors, I fell asleep and slept, dreamlessly this time, for hours.

When I woke, it was late morning, still raining, darkening toward afternoon, judging by the light—or lack of it—at the window, and while I was trying to decide what had aroused me, apart from almost frantic hunger and thirst, the doorbell pealed again.

A spasm of terror went through me. Matthew? One of the coven from last night checking up on me—or coming to see if I was dead or alive? *Well, that was nice of them.* I ran to the window and peered down. I had forgotten that Aunt Sara's window looked down only onto the graveyard, and there was no one there; I ran into the hall and down the stairs, and peering through the leaded panes, saw a little car drawn up at the *porte-cochère* and the welcome face of Claire Moffatt—Colin's partner from San Francisco.

Whatever she was doing here, no one had ever seemed so welcome. I struggled with the bolt, my fingers weak, forgetting that I still wore only my heavy winter bathrobe. At the sight of Colin's friend standing there, solid and real, real and *good,* I felt like breaking out into sobs, and crying till I could cry no more.

"Did I come at a bad time?" she asked. "Colin said you were staying here, and I don't know another soul from here to Innsmouth—oh, I know a few of the locals, but no one I'd call a friend. Brian—Colin said you knew Dr. Standish—said to tell you he intended to check in with you—he got your call yesterday," she said, "only he was stuck on a difficult confinement, out toward Innsmouth, and didn't even get your message until about three this morning. And he's probably sleeping late—he may still be asleep, it's only about eleven. Sara, what's the matter? You look awful! Did I really come too early? You've always been an early bird, at least you always were when you were in school in San Francisco. I thought I'd make some coffee—better than the coffee shop in Arkham. Or I could take you to breakfast, if there's a decent place to go, but—it can't be a hangover, unless you've taken up solitary drinking. Are you sick, Sara?"

"Not exactly," I said slowly. What time was it, anyway? The clock on the wall hadn't been wound; it had stopped at about eight. About eleven, Claire had said. "Come in, Claire, and let me put on some clothes," I said. "I was asleep upstairs, that's why I kept you waiting."

She stepped inside and hugged me in greeting. She was a tall woman, somewhere in early middle age, hair going grey and, just now, wet with the rain that was still coming down hard on the cobbles in the yard.

"Don't think you have to get dressed up just for me," she said. "You can see I didn't." Claire wore her old blue jeans and a grubby raincoat. Under her arm was a paper sack. "I brought along a pound of coffee and a coffeepot; I know you always drink tea, so I thought you might not have any. Do you mind if I go and make some while you dress?"

"Please do." I would be glad to get it, too. This wasn't the time to sit and drink tea; and if I decided to go to the police I'd be glad to have another woman with me. Claire would certainly do that. In San Francisco, she worked on a women's rape hotline, and she'd certainly be sympathetic.

She went off toward the kitchen, and I climbed the stairs. Aunt Sara's portrait seemed to leer knowingly at me as I climbed; *Can you still say you're not a witch?*

I pulled on the first thing that came to hand, a blue corduroy wrap-around skirt and a matching sweater. I sat at Aunt Sara's dressing table to run a comb through my tangled hair; the mirror gave me back my face and I knew why Claire had stared so. My eyes were immense, still dilated, with great dark circles around them; my face seemed blotched and pale. In an attempt to soften the blotched sallowness, I knotted an Indian print scarf, orange paisley, around my throat, hoping it would lend me a bit of color. I tried a little lipstick but it made me look like a painted clown and I rubbed it off again. The smell of herbs from Aunt Sara's dressing table was nauseatingly strong. I picked up the porcelain jar containing the "unguent of Venus" and abruptly hurled it against the wall.

It was a pointless gesture, but it somehow symbolized my rejection of Aunt Sara, this house, and everything in it.

By the time I went downstairs, the good smell of coffee was stealing through the whole house, and in the kitchen Claire, her raincoat off, was making herself at home. She was also making friends with Barnabas. "He's beautiful," she said. "Did you find him here? Was he your Aunt Sara's cat?"

"Heaven knows," I said dully. "Some of the locals have some theories about that. I don't know what to think." He had been no help at all last night. I wished suddenly that he had been a large fierce Doberman.

"Have you eaten anything today, Sara?"

"No. I couldn't get anything down," I said, and she stared.

"What in the world has happened to you? Whatever it is, my

first prescription is *food*. No, you sit still. I make a beautiful omelet, if I do say so myself; it would give competition to any French chef in the business. And I see you still have some eggs—" she stared at the ruins of my last night's supper in the sink. "Hey, this isn't like you, ever since I met you, you've been almost compulsively tidy! Neurotically orderly, and now—Sara, look, I've been kidding you, but if you're really sick—here I am, or shall I get a doctor, or call the ambulance? What's the matter?"

I found myself pouring out the whole thing. Matthew Hay's insistence that I attend their Esbat and my refusal. My attempt to run away, and Tibby's curious maneuvers. Judith Hay, the basket, the drugged plate, the way I'd passed out. Then the nightmarish Witches' Sabbath, the rape . . .

She listened to it all quietly, without comment. When I reached a stopping point she said, "I think you need food and coffee anyhow. Let me make this omelet while you finish." She set a cup of steaming coffee in front of me. "Drink it black, Sara, if you can; I think you need it."

"Do you think I'm crazy? Don't you *believe* me, Claire?"

"I don't know what to think," she said seriously. "I believe you believe it, I don't think you're pitching a yarn—or what is it the kids say—trying to put me on. But I don't believe you went to any Witches' Sabbath, either. Although, God knows, there are such things, and I must say I knew you were in some kind of trouble; that's why I came."

"You knew—what?"

"That you were in trouble; Colin mentioned you were here, and sometime last night I got the feeling you were in some kind of trouble, so I made an excuse—"

Well, maybe she was a witch too. Maybe everybody was and I had just never noticed. Hadn't Fritz Leiber written a science fiction novel about that kind of thing—that all women were witches in secret? Yes, *Conjure Wife,* that was it. The way I felt this morning, I was ready to believe it.

"You always know—what?"

"When someone's in trouble; it's about the only way I'm psychic. Colin says it's a gift; it's how I met him. I'll tell you about it some time. Not now; right now, let me make this omelet; I think you need food." She broke eggs into a bowl and whipped them, while I sipped the black, bitter coffee. It tasted surprisingly good. Claire got down a skillet, poured the eggs into it, deftly flipped them over, folded the omelet and turned it out on a pair of plates.

"Now eat while that's hot."

She slid into a chair across from me and began to fork up mouthfuls of egg. I still thought I'd be too weak to eat, but once I tasted it I realized that I was ravenous. I devoured everything on the plate and accepted a second helping of coffee.

"Feel better now?" She put down her own cup and looked at me.

"A little," I said. "But I do believe part of it happened. A lot of it could have been hallucination, of course; I realized that the hallucinatory parts—the Horned God, the flying—couldn't really have happened; not the way I saw them, anyhow."

"You could have dreamed it all, Sara. Colin said this house was getting pretty badly on your nerves, and remember, you could also be suffering from delayed shock. Losing your whole family like that, inside a few days—"

"No, Claire, I didn't dream it all," I said. "I haven't told you the rest. When I first woke up, I thought it was just a nightmare—the great-granddaddy of all nightmares; a nightmare to end all nightmares. Then I found out that I was outdoors, in the graveyard, with nothing on."

She drew a deep, sharp, whistling breath. "That sounds pretty real. Bad, but real."

"I wondered for a few minutes if I could have walked in my sleep.

But I never have, in my whole life, Claire. And anyway, I've heard that a sleepwalker will do things normally, so if I was going to walk outdoors—and I wasn't drugged—wouldn't I also have put on some clothes in my sleep, too?"

"You're right," she said, "and the fact that you *thought* of sleep-walking means that your reality-testing apparatus is in good shape. My roommate at college used to walk in her sleep. Once or twice a month, she'd get up and dress, lace up her shoes and everything, all completely zonked. She'd even put her key in her pocket. Then I'd tell her it was time to go to bed, and she'd undress, pajamas and all, and go back to bed until morning. She never asked herself any questions about whether it was normal or not." She poured me more coffee and took some herself. "All right, Sara, let's assume that some of it, anyway, was real. The first question is *why?*"

"I thought of a sick practical joke."

"To be that sick, a man would have to be a basket case," she said. "I've met Matt Hay, and he's always struck me as crackers, but not completely nuts. What folks around here call 'a leetle bit touched,' but still not crazy enough to do anything like that for a joke."

"You don't think he's capable of it?"

"Oh, I think he's capable of *anything,* Sara, but that he'd have a good, solid reason; somehow or other it would have to benefit Matt Hay!"

"He could have a reason," I said. "To get me to join them. He told me Aunt Sara was one of them. Their leader." I thought further. "Or even to scare me, after I refused, into selling him this house. Obviously, if this house is overlooking their meeting place, they wouldn't want a stranger, especially an unsympathetic one, living here. If whoever comes to live here puts in electric lights and telephone, maybe digs a swimming pool or rips up the herb garden, or starts a tourist home with guided tours through the quaint old grave-yard—you see what I mean!"

"Oh yes, that would give him a reason, all right," she said. "It sounds vaguely reasonable—" she added, hesitating.

"If it's *not* true, it means I'm completely insane."

"I don't think that for a minute," she said. She drew me toward the lighted window, and I flinched, even dark as it was with the rainy light. She asked, "The light hurts your eyes?" and looked closer. "Yes, they're dilated, even now. As if you'd had atrophine drops in them, or something. Sara, you didn't try to make a pie out of any strange berries, or go blueberrying did you? Last year I ran across some summer people who had gone blueberrying and gotten deadly nightshade instead; you know the berries do look a little bit alike, to anyone who isn't used to them both."

"It grows in the garden," I said. "Matthew Hay told me—oh, God!—that it was an ingredient of the witches' unguent."

"Belladonna," she nodded. "Although you'd have to get an awful lot, and there was probably some other stuff too. It sounds as if you'd gotten *datura stramonium*—what they call locoweed in Texas—and probably a good solid slug of something like LSD or methedrine on top of it all. It's lucky the stuff didn't kill you, Sara. If they had to rely on your getting enough through the skin, they probably put enough on there to kill half the village!"

I brought out the major question, the one that had been on my mind since I first came to my senses naked in the graveyard.

"Claire, was I raped? Or was that part of it all hallucination?"

"Sara, you must know that it's almost impossible to get legal proof of rape on an adult and sexually active woman!" she colored. "Brian did say—I mean, he told me he had been here—with you—proof, yes, but not anything that would hold up in court."

"I don't want legal proof," I said. "I'm not thinking of swearing out a complaint, or taking them to court. I just want to know, for my own satisfaction—just to be sure I'm not losing my mind."

She shook her head. "Even that would be hard—listen, Sara. If, in that drugged state, you believed it—the mind can do funny things with the body. Oh, I could test for traces of semen, or—have you bathed since?"

"Yes. You have to ask? What would anybody do? It was the first thing I did when I was conscious enough."

"Then there's probably no provable trace. As for bruises, soreness—Sara, when I was in training, I saw a demonstration. They hypnotized a student, touched him with an ice cube and told him it was a red-hot iron, and *I saw the blisters come up!* And a person under a hallucinogenic drug is, for all practical purposes, hypnotized. Let me advise you, Sara. Granted I'm not a doctor, but as a good friend: Treat it as a bad dream. *Believe* it was a bad dream. As long as you don't know the objective facts, that's going to be easier on all of us."

There was another thing to think about. (I put out of my mind the memory of Matthew Hay saying: *no woman ever came away from the Black Altar carrying anything she didn't bring with her.*)

"It won't seem so much like a bad dream if about three weeks from now I discover that I'm pregnant, will it?" My voice shook, and I began to sob.

"You poor kid." Her voice was the gentlest voice I had ever heard. "In that case, Sara, we'll assume Brian made you pregnant the other night; he'll probably be glad to get married at the end of the summer."

"I wouldn't do that to Brian," I sobbed. "I'd have to tell him."

"I'll bet it's the first thing he suggests. Your scruples do you credit, though," she said. "If I know that young man at all, it's only a matter of time."

I couldn't answer. I was all unstrung.

Then I'd never know. Was it Brian's child—or the monstrous offspring of gang-rape by some unknown, loutish madman, crazed by drugs and insane ritual?

And Brian himself had said: *I won't follow in Matthew Hay's footsteps!*

Half sick with guilt and fear, I said, "I can't stand the thought of never being sure!"

"I can see how you feel," she said, "I suppose any woman would feel that way. Look here, Sara—do you want to go to the hospital? The emergency room's sure to be open. You could say you were raped—even without proof, they will take it seriously. Or shall I try to call Brian? Or do you have another friend here? Can I do anything for you?"

Before I could get myself together enough to answer, the doorbell rang again.

TWELVE

MORTAL ENEMY

CLAIRE STEPPED TO THE WINDOW, GLANCED OUT ON TO THE BACK steps. "Matthew Hay," she said tersely, "I wonder if he's come to check up? *The infernal gall of him!* You know, if they're checking up—this does lend color to your story, Sara. It goes without saying that I'd like to break his neck. Any woman would."

"Stay out of sight, Claire. Maybe if he thinks I'm alone he'll say something to prove it one way or the other, and then I'll at least *know.*"

"I don't like leaving you alone with him," Claire insisted, looking troubled.

"You think I want to be alone with him? But you'll be there if I need you," I urged, and hesitantly, still reluctant, she withdrew toward the back pantry. I went to the door and opened it, Barnabas nosing inquisitively behind me.

It was, indeed, Matthew. He greeted me with a knowing smile, and at the sight of that smile, my last doubt—if I had really ever had any—fled.

"Well, Sara, now you are one of us. I suppose your memories have returned?"

"Suppose something else," I retorted rudely. "You have a lot of nerve coming here!" I wondered why it had never struck me, before, that behind the rigid lines of his mouth there was sensuality, not the good, healthy kind, but a repressed, evil, sadistic thing. He could talk all day about taking pleasure without guilt and hangups, but *he didn't know the first thing about it.* He was not a liberated, sexually free man; he was a Puritan, over-reacting and carefully trying to commit as many sins as he could, to have the fun of feeling that he was breaking the laws.

For a man like Matthew, if all the taboos had gone from sex, he would probably give it up for the rest of his life. He couldn't seduce me openly, as Brian had, with my free consent. He had to do it in a church, to have the kick of doing something forbidden. Then he had to drug me, or thought he did.

His smile was cruel.

"But you see, I am here, and you haven't attempted to prevent me."

The strange surge of alien emotion, which I had felt once or twice before in this house, surged up. I felt suddenly ten feet tall. I knew I was towering over him. I said, in a harsh voice very unlike my own, "And if I wished to prevent thee, Matthew Hay, all thy feeble spells and tricks would not prevail. Does thee think thee is my equal yet? Not in this world or the next! *I know your name! A-ba-star-no—*"

His face went white, dead white, the color of bleached bone. He took a step backward, half stumbling. "No," he gasped. "No, Sara! I know—"

I lowered my hands, which I had raised as if invoking—*raised to call down the curse,* I thought remotely. I smiled and felt the alien surge *(Aunt Sara again?)* recede. I said, "Just so we understand one another. I don't understand it all yet, but I evidently know enough. Tell me something. How much of that stuff last night was real?"

He grinned, a wicked, sensuous grin. "Just as much of it as you think was real, Sara. I don't know where you went or what happened to you, but there was enough going on down here. But all things considered, you were really flying, weren't you?"

The words struck me strangely. *Flying.* I'd heard hippies on acid talk about flying sensations; it was evidently one of the commonest hallucinations. (Hadn't there even been a case where a hippie, convinced he could fly in reality, calmly walked out a fourteenth-floor window?)

I said, deciding to be subtle to get him to admit it, "It was clever of you, smearing the uh, the——" I had for a moment forgotten the word, not ointment, no—"the unguent on the plate. You might have known that anyone who'd seen the movie *Rosemary's Baby* wouldn't eat anything you sent. That had to be your doing; I don't think Tabitha's capable of it."

"Oh, Tibby's mostly playacting; she's bored," Matthew said. "You told me once, about fifteen years ago, that no one could be a true witch until she was past fifty. A girl Tibby's age can still get everything she wants without witchcraft. But she's coming along very nicely, very nicely; it was a nice little piece of work she pulled on you yesterday when you panicked. Pure suggestion, of course; as you are *now,* you could have brushed her and that damned bird of hers right out from under your feet."

I said, "I notice you didn't think twice about my being poisoned."

He shrugged. "Can't make omelets without breaking eggs. It *worked*: your memory is back. If it hadn't come back, and you stayed a dumb young girl, we'd only have had to get you out of the way somehow or other, anyhow. We had nothing to lose and everything to gain. You're alive, so why are you complaining?"

Claire stepped out of the pantry. She was flushed with anger. "So you admit it, Mr. Hay? You tried to poison Sara? Did you rape her too?"

For a brief moment Matthew was taken aback; he stared from me to Claire in shock. Then he smiled. "Rape? Is that what she told you? It didn't feel much like rape when it was going on." He turned back to me. "All right, Sara, you've had your joke and your revenge. Now get this old hag—whoever she is—out of here, so that we can get down to serious matters."

"Sara asked me to stay here," Claire said, "in the hopes of getting a confession out of you. I guess we've got it."

He threw back his head and laughed, a harsh raucous sound like Tibby's jackdaw. "Confession? What have I confessed?"

"You tried to poison her with your damned witches' unguent!"

"Oh, come, dear lady," Matthew said suavely, with his evil grin, "am I to blame if Sara experiments with her aunt's herbal recipes and makes a small mistake in the quantities? You can't prove anything else."

"And what about last night?" Claire demanded.

"*What* about last night?" His grin was positively Satanic. "I can bring any number of witnesses to prove that I was occupied elsewhere."

"In church, I suppose," Claire suggested.

"As a matter of fact," he said, "I was actually conducting a church service, in full view of my congregation—and it would take more resources than *you* could manage, whoever you may be, to break down that alibi." He turned to me. "Sara, you can amuse yourself as you like, but I suggest that you get rid of her now."

Claire advanced on Matthew, quietly. "I'll go when Sara asks me to," she said. "My impulse is to throw you out—but I fully admit you're bigger than I am."

Matthew did not move. "Sara," he murmured, "this has gone too far for a joke."

"She doesn't want anything more to do with you," Claire said. "Now, damn it, *out!*" Very forcefully, she shoved Matthew toward the door. Matthew wrenched loose. He said, "I suggest you ask Sara herself if she wants you to throw me out. If she wants you to, well, that's her affair. But *you* can't give me orders, and I warn you, if you lay a hand on me—"

Claire took it in stride. All she said was, "What'll you do? Call up the big bad bogeyman, and have him carry me off to hell—or elsewhere? I'm sure you're going there sooner or later, but if you don't mind, I won't join you just yet. Mr. Hay, I don't know who you think I am, or what you're used to, but I assure you, I'm not afraid of you. And I know what Sara wants."

"Do you?" Matthew said. "Ask her."

I stood there between them, strangely torn, strangely unable to speak. Why, oh why, at this moment, should I be thinking that Claire seemed somehow helpless, ineffective? Matthew Hay seemed to waver before me, to be again the great Horned One of last night, huge and filled with power, strength, an animal force . . .

Claire did not glance at me. She simply advanced on Matthew. Matthew said silkily, "I warn you—"

"Go to hell. Go directly to hell. Do not pass go. Do not collect two hundred dollars," said Claire, and she took Matthew's wrist in a fast grip—it looked like *kung fu*—and gave him the bum's rush toward the door. Taken off balance, Matthew stumbled, half fell, plunged against the screen door. It gave under his weight and he fell through, measuring his length on the steps and coming to rest on the walk. He lay there stunned for a moment, then rose slowly to his feet. His face was black and contorted with rage. He shook his fist at Claire.

"You'll live to regret that," he muttered.

"On the contrary," she said. "I've been wanting to try that on somebody, but I didn't want to hurt any innocent bystanders. All those lessons should have taught me *something*. Now get—in very exact terms—the *hell* out of here, fast! Or we'll call the police, if you prefer."

I wished then for Brian's offered telephone. But Matthew Hay didn't know the difference—did he? I might already have had one put in. "And before they get here, I'll come down and give you another lesson!"

"You'll regret this too, Sara," he shouted. He raised his hands invokingly to the sky. "I can be your most loyal supporter and priest— or your worst enemy! It's up to you!"

I was silent, as if frozen where I stood. Matthew turned and strode down the walk and out of sight.

Had I made a mortal enemy of Matthew Hay?

No. He would forgive this too, as he had forgiven so much else, over the centuries.

Claire had her arm around me, laughing, but while she comforted me, a strange part of my consciousness stood back and watched, in amusement. The latest pawn in the old game.

The old ordination service reads, *Thou art a priest forever.* I had been ordained at an altar older that that, older than time itself.

Thou art a witch forever.

I was Sara Latimer—eternally a witch.

THIRTEEN

A WITCH FOREVER

CLAIRE SEEMED HARDLY TO NOTICE MY ABSTRACTION.

"I have a feeling you won't have any more trouble with that bastard," she said, in some satisfaction. "He won't be wanting another lesson. However, I think I'd better take a look round, and keep an eye on some of these people. Maybe some time they'll slip up, and I can make a report to the State Police."

"No!" I said quickly.

"I thought you were the one—"

"Claire, I—" I fumbled for words. I must not destroy her opinion of me. But I dared not alienate her yet. Perhaps, when the time came, I could recruit her to the True Worship, the Old Religion.

As for Brian, I wanted him more than I had ever wanted any young man—and there had been so many. I didn't want to lose him, yet I must protect my own past—and my future, my immortality. I had seen other covens break up in the last fifty years, when too searching an eye was turned on them in the community where they operated.

She was looking at me, puzzled. "Are you all right, Sara? For a moment, when you spoke to Matt, I hardly recognized your voice. He seemed to take it for granted that you were on his side in all this, too." She spun me around, her hands on my shoulders. "You aren't, are you?"

"Of course not," I said. "But suppose we did find something. There's no law against practicing witchcraft, is there?"

"Of course not," Claire said. "But there are laws against rape, and there are laws against messing around with poisons and drugs without proper medical supervision. As long as I'm here, I'm going to have my eye on Matt Hay so hard that he won't be able to spit without me knowing where he does it! I'm not going to rest until I see that guy in a padded cell at Mattapan—or wherever they send criminal lunatics these days—if they send them anywhere; seems to me they're turning them loose too damned often!"

But I had no more time for Claire now. Brian must be recruited to the service of the Horned One; everything Matt had said made that all too clear. The alternative—that he must be put out of the way and deprived forever of the power to harm us—was too terrible to contemplate. *Witches do not love;* but I wanted Brian, physically wanted him, more than I had wanted any man in a hundred years. And it looked as if I had him, tightly sewed up; only now I knew how to make the best use of him, without any of my earlier personality's childish emotions. And I would—if Claire would only get out of my way.

"You'd better go now," I told her. "I—I need to rest. He won't try anything else now. Let's forget him."

"Well, if you're sure," she said hesitantly.

"Oh, I'm sure. He won't be back."

Not, I thought, till I called him—and Claire did not want to know about that.

Standing on the porch, I watched Claire take her leave. I was grateful to her—she had come when I was in shock and badly needed a woman's hand—but Matt would have sent Tibby to me for that if I asked him.

I went and sat down in the old kitchen. What was the old saying? *Youth was too good a thing to be wasted on the young?* Well, a witch had the best of both.

Not too long after that the doorbell rang again. This was turning into a busy day; well, so it should be. Looking out on the porch, I saw Brian's face. My eyes were all right now; but I wasn't ready yet to face Brian. Yet I could hardly send him away again. I pulled the door open, accepted the kiss he took for granted now.

"What's up, darling? I found your message—"

"I'm sorry about that, Brian," I said. "I got the wind up over nothing, that's all."

I had no time to deal with Brian now; I had not yet decided what I wanted to do about him.

"But you *are* all right? Claire said she was over here this morning, and I gather Matt Hay was over here making a nuisance of himself; she said you wanted to talk with me; though she didn't say what was wrong—"

I recalled a line from the old Bible I had found upstairs. *"Beware the strange woman, my son! For her lips drip as a honeycomb, and the words of her mouth are smoother than oil!"* Then I remembered the end of the passage; *but her end is as bitter as wormwood, and sharper than a two-edged sword.*

Brian gave me a disturbed look. "What the hell is that supposed to mean?" he asked in irritation. "I wouldn't have taken you for a Bible-spouter, Sara."

Damn this business of starting again in the body of a silly, naive young girl! (Well at least this time I hadn't had to start as a virgin!) I said meekly, "Oh, everyone picks up a few Bible quotations here and there."

He looked at me oddly, but did not reply. After a few minutes he said regretfully, "Sara, I must go. I came by because I thought you needed me, but if you're all right, I really do have to check my answering service. I meant to, an hour ago. Then I found your message, and got the call from Claire—"

I made no protest when he kissed me and said goodbye; I was tired, and I needed time to think. Not only was Brian a splendid lover, but as a doctor he would be the most valuable of recruits, and far from the first I had brought through my bed to the altar of the Horned One.

With a doctor in the coven we would have reliable access to drugs, and if, as occasionally happened, something went wrong, a doctor could sign death certificates without any trouble and with no one questioning him.

He seemed disappointed when I did not suggest accompanying him, but he only kissed me again, and said, "Yes, you seem tired. Sleep well, love. We'll have to get a telephone in here, so I'm not always rushing off."

Mentally, I answered, *"Over my dead body,"* but I only smiled and said, "All in good time," watching him go out into the rain that was still falling. After a while, the sound of his little Volkswagen started up, and finally faded again, and I went upstairs and slept.

I was interrupted only once, late that night, when the doorbell summoned me downstairs and, holding the lamp high above me, I saw Tibby standing on the steps.

"Come in, Tabitha," I said dryly, "I was expecting you. Is the pupil coming to check on the teacher?"

She said, blinking in the light, "Not for that, Sara. Only to be sure you were all right. If your memory had not come back you would have been in a very bad way. I wanted to make sure you hadn't been too badly hurt. I did look in, earlier in the day, but I saw that you had someone with you, so I didn't stop."

"Kindly of you, Tabitha. I owe you something for your little trick with the jackdaw. That was clever, and since it turned out for the best, I shan't—" I hesitated, "punish you. Not this time. But in future, beware how you meddle! And if you use that bird against me again, you'll be scouting the countryside for a new familiar and end up coming and meekly begging me for one of Ginger Tom's get of kittens!"

She studied me with a curious blend of hostility and old affection. She said, "Don't worry; I know I'm not strong enough to fight you yet, Sara. But the time can still come." He glance was cool, clinically appraising. "I think I liked you better before."

"No doubt thee did," I snapped, "thee could dominate me then, and have Matthew all to thyself. But that time is over now. Keep thy place, Tabitha."

She nodded briefly. She said, "You don't need my help, so there was no reason for my call. I'll go now."

"Do," I said, "but be warned. I am glad thee has seen."

I shut the door in her face, went upstairs, and slept dreamlessly.

For the next few days I watched and listened, trying to assimilate and correlate the flood of memories which kept crowding back.

Three hundred years immortal.

The Dark Ones pay well for what we suffer.

And in the long run?

Eternally?

It's no worse than installment buying; enjoy now—pay later!

Once or twice my old self came up to consciousness; mostly when I was with young Brian. In a way I envied her, that girl I had been, growing up at a safe distance from our doomed heritage and curse, and wished I could return.

No. Having set my feet on the Dark Path, there can never be a return.

Deliberately trying to capture those innocent days, I went into the studio and tried desultorily to finish the illustrations for my book, but the pictures of elves and goblins and fairy cities built of jewels seemed insipid and meaningless to me now, and I finally tore up what I had done. I didn't need the money for the book any more. The Dark Ones care for their own. I would never hunger or need again, for every brother and sister shares his all with the brethren. My part was to provide herbs, and I spent hours in my garden bringing it back from neglect and dark ruin. Seven years of neglect could not be wholly restored in one summer, but it was a beginning.

The word had evidently begun to filter through the neighborhood. Everywhere I went, it seemed that someone made a sign of greeting which I recognized. One night, after darkness had fallen, a young woman, pale and distraught, came to my door. I had never seen her before, but the tale she told was an old one to any witch's ears; five children in four years and her farmer husband too intent on his marital rights to care what it did to her.

I brought her into the garden and plucked the proper leaves with instructions. Yes, abortion was the crime of which we were always accused, because these goody-goody farmers didn't like the idea of losing a potential farmhand when the kid grew up. They talked about God's law; well, so much for their God, if he was a kind of bearded old patriarch who liked the idea of a harried, exhausted young mother having her sixth child nine months after the fifth! After that I gave her some sound advice to keep this from happening again until she was good and ready, if ever, and topped it off with another packet of herbs, drawing a swift male symbol on the paper into which I folded the dried leaves.

"Give these to Obed in his coffee. Mind you don't get mixed up and take them yourself!"

"They won't hurt him, will they?" she faltered.

I said with contempt—how these slave women doted on their masters!—"No. 'Twon't hurt him a mite. Just that when he starts up again at the only thing he's good for, pounding away at you, he'll find he ain't so good at it as he used to be. Might give him a shock and teach him a lesson. A man's balls weren't given to him just so he could fill up the world with a couple dozen bedraggled kids." I waved at the graveyard. "Do what I say, Jessie, unless you want to end up out there, while he runs through two or three other wives at the rate of six or eight kids apiece."

After Jessie had gone, thanking me profusely and finally throwing her arms around me and hugging me and blessing me, I thought with amusement that even Brian would approve of this day's work, if not of the form it had taken; he'd never had any luck, so he said, in getting the local farmers to use birth control! I could do better than that!

My next visitor was completely unexpected; in a strange car, Colin MacLaran.

"I thought I'd be hearing from you before this, Sally," he said, and I remembered he had always called the young girl I both was, and was not, by that name. "Claire told me you weren't feeling quite at your best; are you all right now?"

"Oh yes," I said, wishing he would go; but he was a friend of the young girl, so I made myself be polite to him. "Would you like a cup of tea, Dr. MacLaran?"

"Did you ever know me to refuse that?" he asked in amusement; so I put the kettle on to brew. When it was ready I laid the things out on the kitchen table, and hunted up some cookies to go with it.

"Let me pour," he said, and settled down companionably.

"Oh, by the way, I've gotten myself invited to your Sabbat," he announced, his blue eyes twinkling. "I went to call on Matthew Hay, told him I was lecturing at Miskatonic about Cthulhu and the Elder Gods, backed up a few judicious quotations from *The Necronomicon*—"

Now I knew he was making fun of me.

"*The Necronomicon?*" I asked. "But isn't that the imaginary book H. P. Lovecraft made up for his fiction?"

"Oh, it is; but the point is that *Matthew Hay* didn't know that. He knows a lot less about witchcraft than he thinks he does." Colin chuckled again. "He's accepted *me* as a Great Adept."

Well maybe you are. I knew I should not join with this man against Matthew; but in the long run it would do me no harm if Matthew Hay were made absurd before his deluded congregation. "So you'll be at the Sabbat?"

"I wouldn't miss it for anything."

Something prompted me to say, "Don't underestimate Matthew Hay, Dr. MacLaran." Then I remembered I had always said Colin before. His face tightened; then I wondered if I had imagined it.

"Believe me," he said, a little grimly, "I don't." And he left me thinking, *perhaps he really is a Great Adept—maybe I should warn Matthew.* But I did not.

Some inner urge drew me back to my easel, where I prepared a canvas and began a painting, not knowing what would take place. After a time I realized that it was the dim landscape of the graveyard, filled with eerie shapes, dominated by a great, dark, horned Creature. My work was taking on a strange new dimension of strength and forcefulness, and I could not keep back the impulse to show it to Brian when he came.

"Painting your nightmares now, Sara?"

"You don't like it?"

"I didn't say that. It has an uncanny power. You may be a better painter than I ever suspected, Sara, but it strikes me as—well, unhealthy. A side of you I'd never have suspected."

Yes, I could well imagine that. I said, "I paint what's there to paint."

"And you don't tell me how to be a doctor. Anyway, I do think it's great—and it may be good therapy. Is this house still getting on your nerves?"

I stared at him blankly. What was he talking about? How could my own family home ever trouble me? "I'm not sure what you mean."

"Well, as long as it's no problem," he said, kissed me again and went off. He had been very busy for the last few days with a summer outbreak of influenza, and I'd really seen very little of him. I was content for the moment to be alone with Ginger Tom. He was all the company I needed.

The peacefulness of this intermission could not last. The moon was waning, and the time was rushing on toward the Great Sabbat of Lammastide. I saw Matthew coming and going to Tabitha's house but he was wise enough to let me alone. For the present, Tabitha was welcome to him. But the resting period was almost over and, as all periods of peace must, it ended.

I walked down to Madison Corners for groceries and cat food one morning. Evidently before the younger Sara knew any better, she'd spoiled Ginger Tom by feeding him canned cat food, and as a result he neglected his mousing; I'd heard rustles in the house, and seen mouse traces in the pantry, despite meticulous care. I added mouse-traps to the list as I walked; sooner or later I'd have to have a talk with that cat, and get him back on the job, but right now it wasn't worth the trouble.

I knew, of course, that Matthew and I, and in late years Tabitha, were the brains and the leaders of the coven, the guiding minds and souls, the only ones deeply into mystique or religion. The others, the followers, they were superstitiously hoping to propitiate the forces of nature, or they were attending just because it was the local social thing to do. They might just as well have been shouting at the local gospel or revival meeting, or singing decorous hymns in the Presbyterian church, but it suited me well to keep them away, and at our altar instead. We could use their help, their faith, the worship from which we drew endless, relentless power.

We gave them as much as we took from them, of course. We gave help and counsel, as I'd done to Obed Tate's bedraggled little wife. And at the Esbat—I smiled to myself at the thought that many of the men came, attracted by the wild sexuality and orgies, not realizing that what seemed like an orgy was a drawing down of Cosmic power. Through the energy generated by the passion of two frenzied bodies interacting, the partakers in this sacramental sex tapped an ever-flowing current of the energies of nature.

They didn't care. They were just balling. But I knew, and I used the generated force.

In a very real sense this coven was the life of the community—such life as this decadent part of the world, forgotten by other social services and community institutions, still had. I knew that about half the people I met in this little store—the more energetic half—were my brothers and sisters in the Old Religion. The others didn't matter.

As I ordered my groceries, I thought that unless Brian were recruited, he must be persuaded to leave. (Possibly, if I threw him over, he would go back to Boston.) Brian would give the people around here another kind of focus for their lives, and thus he would threaten the purpose, the very existence of the Old Religion. He would bring Today into this community—and we had a vested interest in Yesterday.

Brian must become one of us—or he must go. The only other alternative was too dreadful to contemplate.

Then I heard a shrill, childish voice behind me:

"Ma, is that the woman you said was a witch? She don't look like a witch, she looks like the doctor's lady friend."

I turned slowly and looked. Annie Fairfield, in her neat print housedress, turned slowly white and clutched protectively at the hand of the small tow-headed boy by her side.

A spasm of rage went through me. I raised my hand, with quiet deliberation, and pointed my finger straight at the boy. Then I turned my back and walked out of the store, laughing to myself.

(The girl I had been could never have done that. But people around here must learn who they had to reckon with.)

Behind me I heard the child double up in a paroxysm of coughing and wheezing. I did not turn. I walked home, smiling quietly to myself. They would learn.

I had expected Brian tonight, and had put a chicken over to stew for fricassee, but he was delayed, and it was almost an hour past the time when I had expected him before I heard his Volkswagen coming up the hill. I was angry enough to try and teach him a lesson, but he looked so tired and worried when he came in that I forgave him for keeping me waiting.

"What's the matter, Brian?"

"Emergency call; the Fairfield kid had asthma, and for a while I was afraid I'd have to rush him in my car to the hospital in Arkham, but he's going to be all right. Damn it, I wish I had a proper clinic and access to an oxygen tent. We're going to have to manage to get *something* for emergency treatment that's closer than Arkham." His face was white and strained. "Every time I have a really close call, I realize all over again what it's going to be like, practicing out here."

"Fairfield. Is that—"

"Yes, that's Annie's kid."

"Serves her right."

"Sara!" He looked honestly shocked. "How can you say such a thing? Just because Annie is an ignorant neurotic, and insulted you, you can't feel sorry for a sick kid?"

"There's no sense in being sentimental about people like that," I said.

He frowned at me and said, "Sara, I think this house is getting to you whether you know it or not. I'd have sworn that kind of comment, that kind of cruelty, wasn't *in you* when you first came here. I wonder if you really ought to stay here."

"Of course I'll stay," I snapped. "I've been here three hundred years and I'm not going to let it fall to ruins now!"

He thrust aside his coat. "I'm not going to quarrel about it with you, Sara. I'm too tired. Whatever's cooking smells good. I hope it's ready to eat."

He praised the food extravagantly, but I was still conscious of the shadow between us. When we had finished eating we fed the scraps to Ginger Tom, although I made a half-hearted protest. "He's getting too fat, he's letting the mice pile up. Cats in this part of the world aren't just pets, they have to earn their keep."

But I didn't make any more protest than that. He was too tired to make any suggestions about going upstairs; after we finished the dishes—he insisted on helping me dry and put them away—he seemed content to sit on at the kitchen table, sipping a last cup of coffee. I had little to say; I was thinking of the best way to suggest to him that he join me in the Old Religion.

"I wish you had a telephone, Sara. I'm on emergency call tonight and I have to stay within earshot of my phone, so I can't stay more than another half hour or so: Cousin James was up half the night last night delivering a baby, and I promised I'd be back by nine so he could get off to bed. You're not listening, Sara?"

I hadn't been; I was thinking that with the Great Sabbat at the next new moon, I'd have about ten days to convince him to join us. But I said hastily, "Of course I was. I just thought I heard something in the backyard."

He cocked his head sidewise. "I don't know. Sara, I wish you'd let me get you a dog."

"Ginger Tom's better than any dog," I said. "He'll let me know if there are any strangers about." I went to the window, followed by Brian. I was not sure, but it seemed that a figure slipped away into the darkness.

Ginger Tom would warn me of a stranger. But would he warn me of the presence of anyone he knew? I was not fully accustomed, again, to the use of the witch-sight, but I felt ill at ease. Matthew Hay had not moved yet, but he was not anyone to forget an insult or offense. He could not move against me—not now. After the Great Sabbat, when he no longer needed me so much, it would be another matter and I must watch myself, but just now I had no particular fears.

Not for myself. But would he move against Brian?

Brian was reaching for his light sports jacket. He said, "I must go, Sara. Cousin James is really pretty old, and I'd like to see him get more rest."

I took a lamp and went with him to his car. A creeping, deadly unease was growing in me.

"Brian, don't go, don't!" I set the lamp down and clung to him.

He kissed me, hard and deep, his mouth closing passionately on mine, but he drew away:

"Sara, you know I have to. You knew what it would be like when you chose to fall in love with a doctor," he said, laughingly persuasive. "You'd better marry me right away and move down into town with us!"

Never! Love is one thing, but I wasn't meant for marriage and domesticity. But I felt so uneasy about him I would not argue that point now.

"Brian, you mustn't go, you mustn't get in that car!"

He looked at me hard-faced, almost in anger. "Don't go psychic on me, Sara. I had enough of that today from Annie Fairfield. She's trying hard to convince me that you're a dangerous woman, a witch. I told her to shut her trap, finally. But it doesn't help when you come on with this kind of neurotic nonsense. Good night, darling. I'll try to see you tomorrow."

He climbed into his car, shut the door firmly and started the engine. I stood, clutching myself in an agony of unease. *What could I do? Oh, what could I do?* As the car rolled away, I stayed there on the steps, frozen, desperate. I listened to the sound of the motor disappearing over the hill.

Then I heard it, what I had halfway expected since he touched the car handle. The sound of the motor changed, somehow; there was a wild squeal of brakes, a strange sound I could not identify, and a hard, shattering crash of metal and glass and machinery.

I snatched up a flashlight from inside the door and ran down the hill. At the foot of the road, where a small bridge led over the creek, made a sharp right turn and began to climb the hill again toward the Whitfield farm, Brian's car had missed the turn and lay canted over sidewise, one fender crushed and the side crumpled in. I think I must have screamed as I ran to the car and wrenched sickly at the handle. Brian was slumped over the steering wheel and there was blood on his forehead, and for a heart-stopping moment I thought he was not breathing.

Then he opened his eyes, dazedly, and I began to breathe again, too.

He said in a stunned voice, "I knew I should have had those brakes checked. They just—stopped working, when I braked for the turn. I'm lucky I wasn't killed. If that door had bounced open when I struck the bridge, I'd have been thrown out and broken my neck."

"Are you hurt?"

"I guess—" he moved, cautiously. "Yes; my ankle is either broken or dislocated. It jammed between the clutch and the brake pedal."

"Brian, what shall I do?"

He thought a minute, his face twisted with pain.

"I hate to have you walking around the countryside in the dark—"

"What could hurt me here?"

"Go past the Whitfields, they don't have a telephone, to the Millard Farm—big green house with the enormous barn behind. Phone Cousin James and he'll drive out here and get me."

The walk in the dark, by only the wavering flashlight, felt strange and haunted. My mind seemed in suspension; I could not think of anything just then except Brian, wedged in the wrecked car. I made my telephone call; Brian's Cousin James told me curtly to wait where I was, and the Millards, friendly, pleasant, aging farmers, offered me coffee and a beautiful piece of deep-dish apple pie, full of sympathy for the strange young lady and for the poor doctor hurt in his car. Mr. Millard offered, as soon as it was daylight, to get his tractor out and haul Brian's car free of the ditch and into the garage in Madison Corners—"No sense, paying one of them tow trucks, they charge you an arm and a leg!" Very soon I saw lights coming up the road and the next hour was too full for thought. Cousin James and Mr. Millard got Brian out of the wrecked car and into the back seat of the older man's car; Cousin James, who turned out to be a sharp-featured, white-haired old man, demanded if I could drive, and when I told him yes, informed me briskly that both he and Brian should not be absent at once from the county, and told me that I could drop him at his—and Brian's—house in Madison Corners, and drive Brian in to the emergency room in the Arkham hospital so that his ankle could be X-rayed and set.

It never occurred to me to protest; it was such a rational arrangement. Brian held my hand in the emergency room, waiting for the X-rays, and told me many times what a help I'd been. He didn't refer to the way I'd foreseen the accident, and his face was so white with pain that I wouldn't even try to say, "I told you so."

The ankle was only dislocated, and when it had been set and taped up with elastic, I drove Brian home and saw him put to bed with some of the codeine the Arkham doctors had given me for him. They had wanted him to stay overnight in the hospital. He wouldn't hear of it, saying Cousin James was too old to be left alone with such a scattered practice. "Sara will drive me for a day or two, if I need it. But I won't need it."

I finally left him sleeping and made my way back to the Latimer house, black and deserted in the pale light of dawn. I was too tired to sleep; I sat in the kitchen, cuddling Ginger Tom on my lap—when, imperceptibly, had I stopped calling him Barnabas? Was that Matthew Hay's doing too? Rage was mounting in me.

Brian was *mine*.

How *dared* Matthew interfere? And with *me?* Until I tired of Brian, no one in this world had the right to interfere with him. Matthew must have tampered with the brakes, and he should be taught a lesson.

I sat, waiting for the sun to rise, and for the showdown with the presumptuous warlock who dared to lay a hand on the Chosen One of his own priestess and witch.

FOURTEEN

A WITCH CANNOT LOVE

AS THE SUN ROSE, A RED AND INFLAMED EYE THROUGH THE LAYERS of cloud, Ginger Tom slipped off my lap and was gone in a flash through the kitchen door. I went out into the herb garden, fragrant in the early dew, and walked slowly toward the graveyard. The ruined church was the place for this meeting, and by choosing the time and place myself I would gain the upper hand.

But before I came through the twisted old iron gates I realized that it was too late for that. Matthew Hay came through the gates, Tabitha at his side, and walked slowly and deliberately toward me. Yielding to necessity, I shrugged and walked between them back toward the kitchen. Giving them the choice of meeting place was a disadvantage, but to protest would be to put myself even further at their mercy. I tried to conceal that I felt afraid. Could I fight them both, if they had joined against me?

Once I could have done so. But after seven years, and still only partially sure of my own memory, my own powers, I did not know. Nevertheless I tried to conceal my sense of defeat and fear.

"How dare you lay hands on a man I have chosen for myself," I stormed. "You have no right! *I know your names!*"

"So you do," said Matthew quietly, "but this is too important for petty revenge. Our very survival as a force here may be at stake. Don't try to work against us, Sara; we all need each other."

Tibby said, "Don't you understand, Sara? The young doctor belongs to your old life; the young girl you were, before you came back to us, was beginning to fall in love with him. You know we cannot love—we must not love. Give him up, Sara. He will only draw you back to what you were before."

Yes, I thought, sick and paralyzed. *I love Brian,* or rather, my girl-self had begun to love him. And a witch cannot love, and keep the tremendous power to manipulate other people's minds and lives.

A person in love is thinking of someone other than herself. The power of a witch comes—at least in part—from a tremendous concentration upon her own will and her own desires—"Positive Thinking" kicked upstairs about a hundred times over. This enormous force of concentrated will-power can tap tremendous energies, but it must be absolutely undiluted, absolutely one-pointed, upon what the witch desires. The slightest thought about the well-being of another and the total self-concentration is broken and destroyed.

This is how the ruthless millionaires make their fortunes; total concentration upon riches and power, and no moment to spare for any other person. Sometimes when they acquired their fortunes they tried to buy women to serve their pride, but they were essentially loveless men.

The legend of Alberich in the Ring of the Nibelungs, then; the ugly dwarf who must renounce love in return for total power, total riches!

And now I must choose.

(*Or had I chosen through all eternity, three hundred years ago? Was I still free to choose?*)

I said, faltering, looking from the tall, cruel man to the small, fair-haired, hard-faced woman:

"Why not let me go? You should be glad if I choose Brian. You at least, Tibby. Then you will have Matthew all to yourself, and no one to contend with you for power and place within the coven."

Tabitha flickered a smile, and I felt that she was wavering; but Matthew Hay said harshly, "A hundred years ago, if you were so rash as to let some sentimental notion come between you and the power you have learned to need as an addict needs his drug—I say, a hundred years ago I would have let you go. Not now. We are too few now. We need you; we cannot afford to lose even one witch of your power."

I shook my head as if to clear it. I said, "Why not recruit Brian to the Old Religion?"

"No. He belongs to the young girl you were. His presence in the coven would always draw you back. What's more, he fancies himself a humanitarian. He still feels obliged to put the welfare of others before his own wishes. Answer me truthfully, Sara; could he take you as I have done, ruthlessly, satisfying himself? And could he leave you free to sate your own desires without caring about his welfare?"

No, I thought. Brian wanted all of me and had made that clear. Even sexually, desire came second to the well-being of one he loved. I had known all along, I supposed, that Brian could never be recruited to our kind of worship. If, following my own momentary desire, I wanted Matthew Hay, Brian would always expect me to think of how he would feel about it, and deny myself. Or—worse—he would "understand" it and permit me to have what I wished, simply because he loved me.

No. He could never be a witch. He could not harm another person for his own desires, he could never put his own convenience before, say, his duties as a doctor.

"You see," said Matthew, "he cannot be one of us. The temptation must be removed. We need you too much, Sara, to let him draw you away. Give him up now, and come back to us, or we will—

remove him. You saw tonight what we could do, it was a warning. Next time it will not be a warning. Next time he will die."

I said harshly, "I still want him!"

"Be sensible, Sara. If you go to bed with him again, can you only desire him, take what you want of him, or will your sentiment get the better of you?"

"If I fight you for him—"

Tibby said, "If you fight us for him, you will be doing it for love of him, and your powers will slowly dwindle; you couldn't save him. Anyway, what do you want from him, what the hell! He's only a man! The world is full of them, and if you want one for your bed, all you have to do is crook your finger. You're young and beautiful and you still have all your old glamour. You've got to let him go, Sara, and if you can't see it, well, we'll have to put him out of your reach. Once he's dead you'll soon realize that a corpse can't give you anything— not pleasure, not power, and certainly not love! Do you need that strong a lesson?"

I felt slowly crushed, defeated. They were right, I supposed. Three hundred years of a will to power told me they were right. And yet—*and yet*—

"Still squeamish?" Matthew said. "All right; we'll make a bargain with you. Come back to us—completely, reserving nothing, the way you know you want to—and we won't insist on his death. We can drive him out of the community, easily enough. But we won't lay a finger on him."

I knew that I had no choice. "It's a bargain," I said. "Lay off Brian and I'm with you."

I had not realized what their plan included. Yet when they told me, I knew it was the only way to save Brian. Further involvement with me meant death for him, for Matthew and Tabitha would certainly carry out their threats. So I let them do as they would.

It was four that afternoon when I heard a car coming up the hill. "Brian," I said, and looked up at Matthew.

We were all upstairs, in the enormous four-poster king-sized bed. I had wondered, when I first came there, why it was so immense, why one old woman should need such a great bed, and so many mirrors in the room. Now I knew, I had been learning all over again why. In the tilted mirror, through the clouds of erotic fragrance, I saw our three naked forms, Tibby slight and delicate, Matthew hard, lean, hairless, lithe as a cat; my own slender body shrouded in clouds of red hair.

I leaned over Tibby, my mouth first finding hers, then creeping down her body, my hands closing on her breasts. My body covered hers, and we writhed together as Matthew, straddling me, drove into me from above. He was hard and tireless and I found myself wondering how he kept his strength after all the time we had spent there together. Tibby's hands played wildly with my breasts, exciting them, as Matthew leaned over me to grip her in a savage grasp, his teeth closing over her nipples.

Downstairs I heard Brian's uneven step and heard him call, "Sara?"

"Up here, Brian!" I called, my voice fading out as Matthew's frenzy mounted, wiping out all awareness from me. At a far corner of my senses I heard him start unevenly up the stairs. *Limping. It must be his bad ankle, still giving trouble.*

I should have gone down.

No. Forget that.

Matthew's great shoulders rose and fell above me, driving with relentless strength, and I heard myself gasping, moaning, pleading and screaming with hungry need. The door was flung wide and just as I exploded into a writhing, clutching wildness, I saw Brian's shocked face white and frozen, dumbstruck, in the mirror.

I waited until my breathing quieted, and then smiled at him, a slow, erotic smile.

"Won't you join us, Brian? There's room enough for us all." I moved my hand lazily over Tibby's lips; she bit the finger lightly and murmured, "Yes, Brian, I've wondered for a long time what's under that starched white jacket of yours."

The door banged shut, blanking Brian's face. I heard him stumbling on the stairs, weaving like a drunken man. The front door slammed; and after a little while his car started up and drove away.

I burst into wild, frenzied weeping, and clutched at Matthew, hurting him with my clawing grip.

"Make me forget!" I demanded. "Make me forget!"

He did.

FIFTEEN

THE BLACK-HANDLED KNIFE

NOW THE TIME GALLOPED TOWARD THE GREAT SABBAT.

I had not seen Brian again. I had not expected to, and to tell the truth I did not really want to. A strange emotion seemed to be clogging my senses. Did I feel guilty? Ashamed? How could I? I had only been finding the one thing that could matter to me now—physical pleasure. I utterly refused to think there had been anything wrong with it; did Brian have any right to think he owned my body, just because I had been willing to take him to my bed? Would I have him keep me for himself?

Hypocrisy! He wanted pleasure from my body for himself, but in spite of his talk about wanting me to have the best, he meant he wanted me to have it only with him! So much for love!

And yet the memory nagged at me; how kind he had been when I was alone, how gentle. How I had enjoyed making plans for the rest of our two lives . . .

Forget that. Only my brothers and sisters in the coven remained and now, in less than a day, I would be confirmed again in my place, this time not drugged and unconsenting, but in full possession of my senses and wits.

I did not flinch from what I knew must be done. Nothing could harm me now.

In the next day or two, around Madison Corners, two or three times I saw the woman—Claire, was it?—who had rescued me the morning after the Sabbat; I owed her something for that, but I had no time for any outsiders now.

One day in town I encountered Matthew Hay in the general store; and he walked with me down the road. Matthew said, "At the Great Sabbat, as you take your place among us, you must demonstrate your freedom from man-made laws. Whenever a former witch returns to her place, this must be done. In the first place, this—which is a crime in mundane society—shows your willingness to place your life in our hands; it is a symbol of your trust that we will never betray you—to do something for which betrayal would mean death."

And I remembered that in each of my lives this had been done, from the first. The black-handled knife on the altar was the memento of this; the only human sacrifice made to the Horned One, at the installment of a returned witch into her place. With it, she would kill, upon the ritual altar, and for that one Sabbat, the living nude body of a woman on the altar was replaced by a corpse. This meant that she could never leave or betray the coven—at the price of being accused and convicted of murder by all twelve witnesses. After, the dead body would be abused by all present; then secretly buried in a place known only to the coven.

I asked, "Who will the victim be?"

"Does it matter?" Matthew asked. "One of the local people, the ignorant ones. They are no loss to the world."

I had to agree. Even Brian had said that maybe it would be better if they all died. *Forget Brian.*

I stopped asking and left it to them. A victim would be provided by the Horned One. It had always been so. It would always be so.

I spent the day before the Sabbat in the upstairs studio of the old Latimer house, painting like one possessed—as perhaps I was. I still have the painting; my only memento of that terrible time. It stands before me as I write, and it still evokes the power to make me shudder, in a frenzy. I have wondered if it is only the memory it brings back, of the horror of those days; but no. Everyone else who has seen the canvas has exclaimed, or shuddered with fear and revulsion at its uncanny power to evoke the old nightmares of the subconscious. And yet it was only a graveyard by the grey astral light, the ground seeming to heave and shudder. In the background stands a lightning-blasted oak, and from one black branch a figure dangles, a figure only lines and black shadows, and yet it is the figure I see every morning in my mirror. And over it all towers in shadow a great Horned Creature, menacing, stooping, enormous . . .

I have told myself a hundred times I should burn the morbid thing. Yet I know it is the only great painting I shall ever make, although even I shuddered when I saw the title in the exhibition catalog last year.

Number 15. *Hanged as a Witch.* Sara Latimer . . .

Just as the sun set, I scrawled my name in the corner of the canvas, and set it aside. It was too early to light a lamp, so I rummaged in one of the empty box-rooms by the grey twilight for what I wanted, and finally found it, packed in fragrant herbs I did not recognize; a long, homespun, hand-woven robe, embroidered with strange symbols in faded silk. I slipped it over my head and felt the atmosphere of it enfolding me.

It is a lie that all witches work naked. (Pure sanity would tell us that a naked witch in winter—and one of the Great Sabbats is at midwinter—would die of exposure.) But it is true that some covens meet naked, or some members come there naked. For nothing of mundane wear can be worn into the magic circle of witchcraft; and in the olden times not all witches had enough spare clothing to keep one garment only for wearing at the meetings. So rather than wear any garment of daily use to a Sabbat, the witch must come naked . . .

Tabitha came for me an hour after sunset, rapping as lightly as a mouse at my door. Wrapped in a great shawl, she looked shrouded and cold, and we did not speak as we made our way slowly across the herb garden, now giving out all its fragrance. (The night was hot! *Why was I aware of the cold?*)

We went through into the graveyard, avoiding the fallen, ruined stones, and as I glanced up, I saw the outline of the great hill beyond, and its strangely topped crest. There was nothing there now but grass where the Whitfield cows grazed; the lightning-blasted oak would have crumbled to dust decades ago. Yet I knew with an inner sight that here in the first of these lives, my body had dangled, lifeless, damned.

Yet here I was . . .

There were pale, ghostly lights visible through the slit windows of the ruined church as I approached, and I knew that the coven had already assembled. And for a moment my steps faltered and I choked with horror. Was it I, Sara Latimer, who walked through a graveyard toward a desolate church where I would commit a ritual murder?

All of them came to a bad end.

For a moment the vision of my father's face swam before my eyes, and I brushed it away, with a little start.

They were dead. For all I knew or cared, they were waiting for me in hell.

I would never really die.

Tibby put a hand under my elbow, but she did not speak. I knew she would not speak at this time unless I first addressed her.

(I had guided her like this, nine years ago. No, that wasn't me! Oh, stop trying to sort it all out. Do what there is to be done. Move with the tides. Accept the inevitability, the forces of cruel nature.)

The night was full of small sounds, crickets moved in the grass, a cicada buzzed with maddening insistence in a tree, far away a fox barked on his nocturnal business and an owl, on almost noiseless wings, moved past us on his cruel hunt; then there was the small, dying shriek of some tiny creature in the grass. Nevertheless the silence oppressed me. I murmured to Tabitha:

"Lights. Have they begun already?"

"Yes. They are waiting for us. You cannot be present at the opening ceremonies until you have been once again made one with us. Have you the unguent?"

I nodded and drew the small jar from the folds of my robe. Tibby twisted it open and smeared a tiny amount on the thin skin of my temples.

Almost at once, although there was a surge of the familiar sickness, it seemed that my night vision improved and the dark graveyard lighted with the curious astral light I had tried to paint that day. Part of me knew that the physical effects were partly the physiological effects of the poison—belladonna's first action was to dilate the pupils of the eyes—yet part of it was real, a psychic opening to unseen dimensions. Beneath my feet it seemed the ground heaved and crawled with the dead, and I shuddered with cold, but this time there was none of the wild delirium; I could, if I wished, distinguish how much was real, how much was the delusion of drugs and excitement.

Even the dim candlelight inside the ruined church hurt my eyes. Briefly I felt as if I were floating. The members of the coven were crouched, chanting, in a circle around the altar, and the naked form that lay there, writhing, just a naked male body, faceless, formless, almost not human to my drugged eyes. I knew now that the great Horned God, crouched over the altar, was Matthew, wearing the animal mask of the God; I knew, too, that the great phallus was tied on and that the crimson at the end was paint, a tradition brought down from the day when one function of the priest of this old fertility-rite had been to sacrifice the virginity of each member, and the blood-colored tip was simply a reminder of this function. I knew this, and yet I shuddered, aware of it all as if I stood before the God of the Woods himself, and knew the terrible nightmarish fear which worshipers of Pan gave his name; *Pan*ic.

Among the figures present, robed like me, I saw one who was both strange and familiar; Colin MacLaran. I asked Matthew, "And this is—"

"Dr. MacLaran, Sara; an adept from the West Coast."

Claire was there too, in a long cloak.

"My acolyte," Dr. MacLaran explained briefly.

"So be it," I said, "if you vouch for her, she is welcome."

The scene wavered before my eyes; the great horned figure wavered as it had done before, now so tiny I could pick him up in my hand, now huge and towering to the vaulted rooftree. The crouching figures were grotesque, their faces assuming strange animal contours. I was alone; Tabitha had slipped away to her place in the circle. The smoke of the incense was choking me! Matthew—or the God— slipped a knife into my hand. Not the white-handled knife of bone, for cutting leaves and roots, for making willow wands, not the knife for the bright side of the witch-woman, to help and to heal, but the knife with the handle of black iron.

The knife of the sacrifice.

I moved without volition toward the altar. I saw the naked body there, the crimson cross marked on his heart with the blood of some warm-blooded thing. I raised the knife.

And then the area spun before me. The faceless, bodiless form before me took on contours I knew, became a face and body known intimately, beloved, known, passionately remembered:

Before me on the altar, bound naked and helpless, fettered with long cords, lay Brian Standish!

The chanting wavered to a frenzy. The smoke of the incense and the fire made me dizzy. I raised the knife.

I brought it slashing down!

But not to his throat!

With a long, single slash, I cut the cords binding him. As he leaped swiftly to his feet, I found my voice and shrieked.

"Run, Brian, run! Get away and call the cops!"

Matthew Hay reeled back from the altar, with a wild, harsh cry, the cry of a foiled beast. My head still spun, but I felt the madness slowly draining out of me. I watched, paralyzed, as Brian came to life. He seized Matthew with one hand, ripped off the horned mask, and his fist shot out. I heard Matthew Hay's front teeth crunch and break under that terrible blow, and he went down, sprawling, knocking the incense pot over.

Brian leaped back; I backed away. He thrust me behind him.

"Run!" I begged. "It's too late for me! Get away!"

"Over my dead body," he muttered, and turned to face Matthew, who said grimly, "That can be arranged."

Matthew had risen and was advancing, howling like a wounded bull. Brian shouted, a harsh, high cry, and leaped at him. With all his strength he struck, a karate chop straight to the neck, and Matthew Hay fell as if poleaxed.

He must have been dead by the time he hit the ground, his neck broken at one blow.

I heard a high, wild scream from Tibby, and saw her run forward, shrieking, to try and raise Matthew in her arms, but Brian tugged at me and we ran. The other members of the coven were still staring in drugged shock, and we realized we'd better get well away before they roused themselves.

We stopped only briefly in the Latimer house to grab some clothes for Brian before running down the road to the Millard farm to telephone the State Police. Still half-drugged, I made a statement; after a while I saw red-lighted police cars converging on the old church.

Brian told me, over a hasty breakfast, what had happened.

"I received a message from you," he said. "It was full of apologies for the other day—" he looked away. "You said that Matthew had hypnotized you and made you do it. Was that true?"

"Yes," I said firmly. I knew now that I had begun to renounce any thought of the coven when I met Brian, that—Aunt Sara?—was gone forever. *A witch cannot love.*

I love Brian.

Therefore I am not a witch.

"Anyway, the letter begged me to come after dark and take you away, and when I came someone hit me over the head; when I woke up I was tied and gagged on that altar. Then I saw you coming, and when you raised the knife—well, I was pretty scared."

I clutched at him and he drew me into his arms and gave me a long kiss. "I think I knew you couldn't have done it."

Then we had to make a statement. Matthew was dead, but it had been obvious self-defense and I was there to testify to it. Anything the others might say was invalidated because the police had found them still drugged and their testimony would therefore not be acceptable.

Tibby, I knew, would never make a statement. When they found her by Matthew's body she was motionless, clutching him mindlessly until they had to pry her away by main force. I have heard that she has not spoken a rational word since; she is still in a locked ward at Mattapan. I still regret Tibby. Her only trouble was that she was so much cleverer, so much more wasted here, than most of the others she knew. In a strange way, I think I loved her, too.

When it was all settled, Brian took me to his Cousin James's house. Then we told the whole story—but only to Colin. James wasn't ready for it.

"We'll be married right away," he said. "The coven can never start up again, with Matthew and Tibby—and Aunt Sara—all gone. Without leaders, they'll either disband, or else keep gathering out of habit, but whatever they do will be no more harmful than a drinking party and sooner or later that's what it will turn into. As for the old house on Witch Hill—shall we sell it, or have it torn down and build a new house on the property?"

"It doesn't matter," I said. "It's just a house now. Aunt Sara's gone forever."

"If she was ever there," Brian said skeptically, "and the whole thing wasn't shock and reaction. You went through a lot, Sara."

"Whichever it is, it doesn't matter. Tear the house down, or let it fall down, I don't care. There's nothing there I want, except one painting. And Barnabas."

But when Brian and I went to collect him, we called, and hunted, and put out tempting bits of liver, but there was no sign of a yellow cat. Barnabas, Ginger Tom, or whatever he was, had gone back to wherever he had come from, exactly as if he had really been Aunt Sara's cat, returned only while he still believed I needed or wanted a familiar. I never saw him again.

I have never owned another cat.